HOW DO YOU FREE A CAGED BIRD?

Michael Emond

Copyright & Content Warning

This is a work of fiction, and any resemblance to real-life events and figures, living or dead, is purely coincidental.

THIS BOOK CONTAINS THE FOLLOWING SUBJECT MATTER THAT MIGHT BE UNCOMFORTABLE FOR SOME READERS:

- Descriptions of intense violence and gore
- Suicide
- Explicit language and suggestive dialogue
- Other dark and intense emotional themes

READER DISCRETION IS ADVISED

Copyright © 2026 by Michael Emond
All rights reserved.
No portion of this book may be reproduced in any form without written permission from the publisher or author, except as permitted by U.S. copyright law.

ISBN: 979-8-9933034-3-7

Dedication

This book is dedicated to the many who are left to rot in favor of the needs of the few.
Human life is priceless.

Chapter 1

Late at night, at an abandoned warehouse that was being used for a drug smuggling operation, a wounded man trembled in fear on the ground. A knife was plunged deep into his thigh, having narrowly missed his femoral artery. The bodies of his comrades littered the floor. Each one of them had at least a single knife precisely thrown at vital points that would kill the intended victim within a few minutes at most. The smuggler attempted to crawl away, desperate to cling to life as the smell of fresh blood lingered in the air.

"Do you have to struggle so much?" a man's voice called from the darkness, tired and mildly annoyed.

A slender man with long dark red hair and cold green eyes stepped out of the shadows and into the moonlight. He wore a black double-breasted suit, a bandolier strapped to his leg bearing a great many throwing knives. He sauntered towards the wounded smuggler, brandishing one of his many blades.

"I don't like drawing out someone's pain longer than I have to, so that's why I always try to kill a target nice and fast. If you struggle, I can't quickly put you out of your misery."

In a fluid motion, the man flipped over his prey. The smuggler thrashed as if he were a defenseless tortoise stuck on its back.

"Please! Let me go!" The Smuggler cried. "I'm just a grunt! A nobody!"

"Sorry," the man replied curtly, "My contract was pretty clear. 'Leave no survivors.'"

The moonlight glistened off the man's knife.

"Somebody wanted your boss and his whole drug operation dead, and was willing to pay good money to get it done. I got bills to pay, and I don't have the luxury of leaving a job unfinished. Oblivion sends their regards."

The smuggler's eyes widened.

"You!" he cried. "You're the Black Bird of Death—"

The smuggler was instantly silenced by a knife thrown into his jugular. The light left his eyes before he even had the chance to choke on his own blood. The assassin let out an exasperated sigh now that his job was finished. He rolled up his sleeve, checking his watch for the time.

"Damn it, another late night. I'm gonna get an earful from Lily later…" he muttered to himself.

Deep within the criminal underworld existed a professional assassin who even the most hardened of kingpins and crime lords spoke of only in hushed whispers. A phantom who single-handedly brought entire heavily-armed crime organizations to their knees, leaving behind knives in all of his victims like a crow that had molted its feathers. The paid assassin they all called…

The Black Bird of Death.

Leon Graves. Age twenty-four. A hitman for the criminal organization Oblivion, code-named Raven. Leon cared very little for his infamous moniker, believing it to be over the top and childish. While many would consider this prodigy an assassin of unparalleled skill in the craft, the reality was that murder-for-hire was only a means to an end for Leon, and nothing more. After he quickly departed the dock warehouse without being seen, Leon headed to the nearest subway station, discarding his bandolier with unused throwing knives into a trash can that would be discreetly disposed of by an Oblivion handler disguised as a city sanitation worker.

***

Mercifully, the site of Leon's latest contract was within a reasonable distance of his apartment, and he finished his job just in time to catch the last train. He had an entire train car to himself as he sat down, mentally drained from his assignment. As the sound of the tracks clacked beneath, Leon reached behind his neck and let his messy red hair down, his shaggy bangs partially obscuring both his eyes. He took a deep breath, releasing it slowly as he tried to relax his shoulders. Leon always hated his work. Every job left him feeling dirty in a way that he could never wash away, and each time he came home from carrying out a kill, it left him feeling broken and hollow.

Still, his organization paid good money for a successful contract, especially for a killer of his caliber. Leon remembered how he used the money from his first job to pay four months' rent and to treat his younger sister and brother to their first dinner out since they could remember. Leon dropped out of high school to provide for his family after their mother died. As long as it was for them, he would do anything he had to do to put food on the table and keep a roof over their heads, no matter how morally dubious or underhanded. The Black Bird of Death thought it better to keep both of his younger siblings in the dark concerning the true, gruesome nature of his profession, knowing full well that they'd object wholeheartedly to the horrors he subjected himself to. For that reason, Leon told them both that an estranged friend of their father's had reached out to him to work as an administrative assistant at a pharmaceutical company. Given how Leon had initially stumbled into the world of murder-for-hire, it wasn't too far from the truth. It was better for everyone involved that his family remained unaware of how he made his money. Considering the only resignation Oblivion accepted was death, Leon didn't exactly have the luxury of quitting his job, no matter how badly he wanted to.

It was all fine and dandy in the end. Leon was simply doing what he had to do to get by, and that was all there was to it. As far as he was concerned, the Black Bird of Death was paid by vile and shitty criminals to kill other criminals who were equally as vile and shitty. They all deserved to die, and he was simply profiting off their greed and bloodlust, as any good capitalist would. That's what Leon tried to tell himself anyway. He knew deep down that one day, when everything was said and done, he'd see them all in Hell sooner or later.

***

It was almost midnight by the time Leon returned home. He unlocked the deadbolt to his two-bedroom apartment, tired and ready to go to sleep.

"About time you got back," a girl's voice called.

A girl, nineteen years of age, sat on a stool at the kitchen island with various notebooks and a large economics textbook sprawled out across the surface as she studied for an exam. She was petite, with messy chin-length red hair. From behind a pair of glasses with thick black frames, peered piercing green eyes that were similar to Leon's.

"I'm sorry, Lily. Things were hectic at work again," Leon apologized. "Had another all hand's on deck situation."

"It's always something... Isn't it?" Lily scoffed.

Lily closed her textbook.

"I left dinner for you in the microwave," she said. "Nothing fancy, just some penne pasta and a red meat sauce. Jamie already went to bed."

Leon sat down at the table across from Lily.

"Thank you," he said in a tired whisper.

Lily bit her lip, looking at Leon and back down to her lap.

"Something wrong?" Leon asked.

Lily crossed her arms, glancing away from Leon. "Jamie and I aren't little kids anymore, you know…" she complained. "You don't have to do everything yourself. I could get a part-time job, so you don't have to work late so—"

"We've been over this," Leon interjected. "I want you and Jamie to focus on school, so you both can get good, stable jobs and be able to fend yourselves one day."

"But I—"

"I'm not bending on this."

Leon smiled weakly, gently placing his hand on Lily's shoulder.

"I'm sorry," he said. "I'm really thankful to have my lil' sister care so much about me, but you're already doing more than enough keeping things at home afloat between the cooking and housework."

Leon's eyes twinkled as Lily met his gaze.

"I'll be okay. I promise," he assured.

Lily stood up, letting out an exasperated exhale while she picked up her things. "Fine," she relented. "Just promise you won't overdo it."

"I promise I won't overdo it," Leon replied wryly.

Lily rolled her eyes, giving a quiet chuckle to herself.

"Liar…" She muttered.

Leon threw his hands up in the air, playfully admitting defeat.

"You know me too well," he declared.

Lily walked to her room.

"Night, Leon," she said. "Don't stay up too late."

Lily closed her bedroom door, leaving Leon alone in silence once more. Leon placed his elbow on the kitchen table and rested his head in his hand as he stared wistfully off into space. Lily was starting to look more and more like their mom every day. Leon was certain that if their mom were still around, she'd pester Leon about needing to rely on other people the same way his younger sister did just now. To be fair, he didn't take pleasure in pushing away his family or working late into the night. However, it was better this way. As long as he could potentially give Lily and Jamie a brighter future, it was all worth it. Keeping them out of the loop was the only way for him to keep them safe from the grizzly world he had become entangled in.

Leon went and changed into a pair of sweatpants and an old T-shirt, hanging his suit jacket and pants on a rack next to the couch. He quickly ate the dinner Lily had left for him before going to pull out the sofa bed. He fell onto the mattress, mentally drained. He rolled onto his back, staring at the ceiling as his eyes adjusted to the darkness once more.

"If only you knew, Lily," Leon whispered to himself. "I'd give it all up in an instant if I could."

He closed his eyes, fatigue finally starting to win out over his conscious and guilt-ridden mind.

"I'm sorry I'm such a crappy big brother..."

Chapter 2

Leon awoke early the next morning to the sound of a kettle whistling on the stove top. He sat up, the back of his hair matted, and his eyes heavy as he slowly came too.

"Good morning!" a boy's voice called.

Leon let a large yawn, wiping his eyes with the side of his left hand.

"Morning, Jamie..." He groggily replied with a drowsy groan.

Jamie was seventeen and a junior in high school. Leon's younger brother had short dark red hair that was almost chestnut brown. Despite being the youngest in the family, he had grown to be a few inches taller than Leon, and his hazel-colored eyes sparkled with an energy and sunniness that both his older siblings had lost long ago.

"Here. I made you some coffee," Jamie said, handing a mug of hot instant coffee to Leon.

"Thanks..." Leon replied, still in a slight half-asleep daze.

He took the mug from Jamie, sipping some of the coffee and accidentally singeing the tip of his tongue.

"Ugh... I'd kill for five more minutes of sleep right now..." he whined.

Jamie let out a small laugh. "You were never a morning person," he teased.

"Cut me some slack," Leon complained. "It was another late night. I didn't get home until about midnight."

"Yeah, yeah, I hear you," Jamie scoffed. "Thanks for working as hard as you do, as always."

Jamie poured the mug of instant coffee he had for himself in a thermos.

"By the way," he said. "My basketball team's trying to raise money for new uniforms, and some of my teammates' moms got together to arrange a bake sale this Friday during our home game. I don't wanna put more and your plate since you're always so busy all the time, but they're asking for donations from everyone, and—"

"It's alright, I got you covered," Leon interrupted with a content smile. "It's been a while since I got to bake anything. It's nice to have an excuse to do it now and then."

"Thanks! You're the best!" Jamie chimed. "I don't think I've ever seen you happier than when you were making or eating a cupcake."

"Only an absolute psychopath would be unhappy when cupcakes are involved," Leon joked.

Leon took a gulp from his coffee, finally perking up a little from the caffeine.

"Is everything going okay at school otherwise?" he asked.

"Yep," Jamie replied. "Mostly A's and B's so far for the semester."

"You're almost halfway through your Junior year. Time certainly flies," Leon mused. "Have you given any thought to where you might want to go to college?"

Jamie started packing up his book bag.

"No, not yet," he replied. "I'm trying to figure it out, though, I swear."

Jamie slung the strap of his book bag over his shoulder.

"I've heard some recruiters are attending my next few games, so hopefully I'll be able to get some leads on a sports scholarship."

Leon finished off his coffee.

"As long as you stay on top of it," he urged. "Keep up the good work, Jamie."

"I will," Jamie called as he headed out the door. "Don't forget about the bake sale, okay?"

"I'll go shopping first thing I get off work today," Leon called back. "Have a good day!"

Jamie closed the door behind him, leaving Leon by himself once more. He wondered how long it'd be before he received his next contract from Oblivion, desperately hoping it wouldn't interfere with the promise he had just made to his little brother.

***

After Jamie left, Leon set out to get himself together for the day. He had a small breakfast of a toasted bagel with crunchy peanut butter and a glass of skim milk. Not long after, he heard Lily leave for her morning classes while he was in the shower, and he now had the apartment to himself. After making the sofa bed and putting it away, Leon sat down and took a lint roller to his suit.

When it came to assassination, black and red were the best colors to wear when on the job. Because his preferred MO was killing unsuspecting targets in the dark, Leon favored the color black, as it was both suitable for hiding in the shadows and for concealing blood stains. Formal attire such as this was also helpful for both blending in the city as a low-level businessman and all the better for keeping up appearances with Jamie and Lily. That said, as practical as blacks and charcoal slate grays were for Leon in his chosen profession, darker colored clothing didn't perform anywhere near as well when it came to concealing rogue lint and the like, a petty frustration that annoyed the Black Bird of Death to no end at times.

The phone in the kitchen rang. Leon set down his lint roller and gently brushed off his suit jacket with his hand before placing it on a hanger so he could answer it.

"Hello," he greeted.

A brief moment of silence echoed on the other end of the line before the caller said anything.

"Quote the raven nevermore," a woman's voice quietly spoke through the speaker.

The call cut off immediately. Leon hung up the phone, narrowing his eyes.

"No rest for the weary, I suppose," he quietly thought aloud in a tired moan. "I wonder who I'll be sending to the grave this time around..."

***

The Final Exit Cafe. Publicly, it was known as a small chic and expensive coffee shop tucked away in a city alley. The reality, however, was that it was yet another "business" owned and operated by Oblivion, Leon's employer and a criminal organization that essentially ran a monopoly on murder-for-hire. Despite the relatively dim lighting, the ornate tables and wall ornaments would have called to mind some swanky cafe from Italy or France. It was the kind of place you'd expect an affluent European businessman to take a lunch meeting that would go on for about two or three hours.

A slender young man who looked to be in his mid to late twenties stood behind the counter, reading a newspaper. He had a pretty face and cleanly cut blonde hair, his neatly parted bangs styled ever so precisely to perfectly frame his hazel colored eyes and delicately chiseled jawline. While he wore a white collared shirt and apron, as you would expect from a waiter, he was pretty enough that high-end designer label clothing you'd find fresh off a runway would have been better suited for him.

Leon entered the cafe, once again donning his suit and having carefully tied up his hair so that it would not fall in his face. The man behind the counter set down his paper, flashing Leon a friendly grin that didn't reach his eyes.

"Hello there, Raven," he greeted, his voice almost lyrical. "Can I make you a cup of coffee? Get you something to eat?"

Leon sat down at the counter. "Only someone with a death wish would eat or drink something prepared by you, Viper."

Viper crossed his arms, tilting his head coyly.

"So cold," he replied dryly. "I'm just trying to be nice."

"You? Nice? Now's a scary thought…" Leon quipped.

Viper chuckled.

"You know, poison doesn't have to be so frightening," he mused. "If you microdose properly, you can develop a helpful resistance. I can help you set up a regimen if you—"

"Hard pass." Leon interrupted, rolling his eyes. "I swear to god, if you start rambling on about microdosing or fangirling over some neurotoxin again, I might just have to stab you."

"Oh, how scary," Viper mused mockingly. "I suppose I should watch my tongue then."

Every interaction Leon had with Viper was always about as pleasant as getting a cavity filled. Granted, Leon always hated having to deal with his fellow agents at Oblivion in general. Viper was an intelligence agent and an assassin specializing in the use of poison. Whenever the Black Bird of Death got a new contract for a kill, Viper would be the one to give him a formal briefing regarding the operation to take place. Leon had at one point heard a rumor that this vile two-faced snake was actually the scion of a large pharmaceutical company that was a front for an old and prestigious clan of assassins, and that he had joined Oblivion to cozy up to the big shots who headed the organization. Despite his obsession with poison, Viper was one of the more well-adjusted assassins out in the world. If you wanted to excel at information gathering and brokering the way Viper did, you needed to be able to put on a charming facade and lie through your teeth as easily as you would breathe.

"Undertaker will be here shortly to give you your next contract," Viper said. "We won't be able to get to the finer details until Intelligence finishes collecting its data, though."

"Whatever…" Leon scoffed, looking away from Viper.

Leon restlessly tapped his middle finger against the countertop over and over again, wondering why Undertaker was taking so long.

"You know, I actually heard an interesting rumor," Viper said.

"Not interested—"

"This one's about you, though," Viper chimed,

Leon silently scowled at Viper.

"Rumor has it, well, a small-scale whisper anyway, is that the Black Bird of Death supposedly joined Oblivion to provide for his family."

Leon remained silent, his eyes cold.

"It'd be an honest shame if you did have a family chaining you down, Raven," Viper said. "If you did have some normie loved ones holding you back, I'd suggest ending their miserable lives so you can kill to your heart's content."

Leon's eyes flickered.

"Who's to say. Everyone has their reasons for joining Oblivion, after all," he replied. "You have assassins who were born into murder like it was a family trade, psychopaths who figured out how to get paid doing what they love, desperate nobodies with nowhere else to go, and so on."

Leon gave Viper a dirty look.

"That said, I personally think it would be a shitty idea to kill the loved one of an assassin."

"Oh, and why's that?" Viper asked.

This time, it was Leon who flashed a friendly grin that didn't reach his eyes at Viper.

"If an assassin had someone they truly cared about, and something were to hurt that person," he explained. "Then I'm sure that assassin would find the party responsible and make them pay…"

Leon's voice lowered an octave, almost guttural and reminiscent of a growl.

"**Dearly,**" he added.

Viper sneered.

"Hmph. You have a point. Broadly speaking, making an enemy of someone like that does sound like a terrible lapse in judgment when you put it that way," he said. "Of course, this was all hypothetical, was it not?"

Leon glanced at the cafe door with an annoyed pout, wondering to himself what the holdup was with Undertaker.

"Yeah," he replied bluntly.

***

A few minutes passed after Viper and Leon's exchange. A hush filled the room as Leon brooded and Viper polished coffee mugs behind the counter. There was nothing more for Leon to do but wait. Undertaker was, more or less, the acting CEO of Oblivion. While many powerful and influential big shots pulled the strings and kept Oblivion functioning, Undertaker was in charge of maintaining the organization's continued operations and, for all intents and purposes, considered Leon's direct superior. If someone like Undertaker took the time out of their day to schedule a meeting with you, you showed up there and waited for them, no questions asked. That was the way of it. Undertaker would say, "Jump," and all those beneath him would ask, "How high?"

The door to the cafe opened, and a sullen woman in a charcoal colored pantsuit escorted a man inside. The man was tall, lanky, and imposing. His head was shaven, and he had sharp features that would remind some of a gargoyle. He wore a custom-tailored Italian suit, the quality of which was worth more than some people would earn in their entire lifetime. The woman who stood by him was pale with silvery hair and bleached eyebrows. Her eyes were cold, resembling those of an old antique porcelain doll, which evoked a gloomy stoicism that made her appear all the more gaunt and intimidating.

Leon stood up, and both he and Viper placed their hands to their sides like soldiers reporting to their commander.

"Sir!" they both greeted in unison.

"At ease," the man said, his voice soft-spoken but powerful.

Leon and Viper relaxed their posture.

"Can I get you anything, Undertaker sir?" Viper asked. "Coffee? Tea? Scones?"

"I appreciate the sentiment, Viper, but Styx will handle preparing the refreshments, as usual," Undertaker replied.

The woman, Styx, nodded her head in silent affirmation.

"Go ahead and close up, and make sure we don't have any rats trying to eavesdrop on our conversation," Undertaker ordered.

"Understood," Viper said, bowing his head.

Undertaker glanced towards Leon.

"Come, Raven," he said, gesturing for Leon to sit down with him at a nearby table.

Leon sat down across from Undertaker at a small table in the center of the Cafe. Viper had locked the front door, flipping the sign on the front to say "Sorry, we're closed," before shutting the blinds in the windows and vanishing to a back room. Styx returned to Undertaker with a tray holding two mugs of coffee, placing a mug in front of him and Leon. Undertaker held out his hand, and without a missing beat, Styx pulled a box of cigars and a lighter from her coat pocket, deferentially handing one of them to her superior. Styx handed him the lighter, which he used to light the cigar before placing it into his mouth. He took a hit from his cigar, handing the lighter back to Styx as he did.

"You did well with your last contract, Raven," Undertaker said, letting a puff of smoke. "Our client was more than pleased by the handiwork of the Black Bird of Death."

Undertaker took out a large envelope from his coat pocket, heavy from the amount of cash inside.

"Your share of the commission, as always."

Undertaker slid the envelope towards Leon.

"Thank you, sir," Leon said.

Leon spoke with a formal professionalism that was about as warm and inviting as an old tile floor in a hospital ER waiting room.

"Styx, the details of Raven's next contract, if you would," Undertaker ordered.

Styx nodded, finally acknowledging Leon's presence.

"A group of defectors from Oblivion has banded together and set up shop in an abandoned ghost town forty miles from here," she said, her voice a monotone whisper. "You are to collaborate with fellow Oblivion agent, code-named Bullet, and silence every last one of them."

Undertaker took another puff of his cigar.

"There is no client for this contract, as it is an internal operation," Undertaker explained. "I'm sure you recall Oblivion's policy regarding those who abandon, betray, or wish to leave the organization?"

"'The abandonment or betrayal of Oblivion is rewarded with death,'" Leon quoted. "'Refusal of a contract is tantamount to betrayal. The only formal resignation Oblivion recognizes is death.'"

"That is correct," Undertaker said.

Undertaker exhaled, savoring the scent of the cigar and taking another puff.

"This contract is not only to punish those who have the audacity to bite at the hand that so generously feeds them, but also to serve as an example to those who might dare do the same. All of this must be done so that order is maintained within the organization."

Leon had heard many things about Undertaker during his time with Oblivion. From what he had gathered, Undertaker achieved his post roughly ten years ago, and many rumors suggested that he bribed and killed his way to get there. Most only ever spoke of it in quiet gossip away from prying eyes and in passive-aggressive subtext, but popular opinion within the illegal conglomerate considered Undertaker to be a petty control freak. He was wealthy, powerful, and above all else, valued absolute obedience. As a result, no one ever questioned Undertaker's orders, or at least did so and lived to tell the tale. The Black Bird of Death knew many horror stories about those who earned the ire of Undertaker and how they had everything they cared about utterly demolished before the tyrannical CEO of Oblivion ultimately placed a contract on their heads.

In short, Leon believed it was for the best to keep his head down and stay in his boss's good graces at all times. As long as he got paid and he could give Jamie and Lily a chance for a better life than his own, Leon was content to do as he was told, choking down all of his complaints and misgivings he would have had otherwise.

Styx quietly cleared her throat.

"Pardon my interruption, sir, but we have other appointments that require your immediate attention."

"Very well," Undertaker replied, almost with disinterested boredom.

Undertaker stood up, dropping his used cigar in the coffee mug in front of Leon to put it out.

"Viper will reach out to give you details of the operation at a later date," Undertaker said. "Do not fail me."

Leon stood up, bowing to Undertaker.

"It will be done, sir," he assured.

Chapter 3

Later that day, at an underground training facility, Leon readied his knives for target practice. Oblivion owned and operated countless of these training facilities across the country, often set up in old abandoned warehouses or underground bunkers where legal ownership had gone to a bureaucratic red tape hell for one reason or another. These establishments were both used as a location to assess potential recruits and for field agents to practice their craft. Each facility was equipped to handle physical training, weapons training, target practice, weapon maintenance, and so on. For an assassin, the slightest mistake on the field or the most minute failure of their tools could easily lead to death on the job, or worse yet, failure to complete a contract. Diligent training was a necessity for every professional killer, and the Black Bird of Death was no exception.

Leon's specialty was covert infiltration, guerrilla combat, and stealth. Killing targets in the dead of night, surprise attacks, and discreetly silencing a mark in a crowded area, you name it. This was among many reasons why Leon preferred knives as his tool of the trade. A knife could be concealed on your person to slip through a crowd as easily as the blade could slide between a target's ribs. His simple and efficient weapon of choice could be used to kill unwitting targets who had dropped their guard, thrown from a distance into a target's major arteries, to quietly slit a target's throat under a shroud of darkness, and so on. To Leon, a knife was as versatile as it was effective.

Leon wore an old t-shirt with gym shorts, wiping light sweat from his brow as he readied a knife to throw. He had already finished the bulk of his standard regimen, having run three miles, three sets of fifty sit-ups, two sets of fifty squats, and two sets of forty push-ups. Compared to the grueling training his father had put him through as a kid, his current routine was child's play. A training dummy was set up roughly fifteen feet away from him, with a variety of targets that were placed on it to mimic the placement of vital veins and arteries in the human body.

Leon's eyes gauged each target like a bird of prey honing in on a helpless rodent. He steadied his breath to a point of silence where you'd sooner hear the sound of a safety pin fall on the floor off in the distance. He had one throwing knife readied in his left hand, and four more on a small fold-out table by his right. Leon quietly breathed in and out, clearing his mind of all distractions. In a quick flurry, Leon threw each knife, one by one, at the training dummy. All five flung weapons struck their target's bullseye, blade first, in rapid and rhythmic succession without missing a single beat.

"I see you're still quite the crack shot," a woman's voice called from behind Leon. "There's nothing more beautiful to me than a bullet piercing a brain, but the way you throw a knife comes pretty damn close."

Leon turned around to see a woman carrying a metal briefcase standing behind him. Her pitch-black hair was cut in a short, fashionably asymmetrical bob, and her smooth alabaster skin was complemented by the ruby red lipstick on her lips and subtle eyeliner around her bright brown eyes. The maroon trench coat she wore was carefully tailored to perfectly accentuate her figure.

"Something I can help you with, Bullet?" Leon asked curtly.

"Oh, I just came to say 'hi,'" she teased.

Leon rolled his eyes.

"Then goodbye," Leon said, getting ready to step away to retrieve his knives from the training dummy.

"Oh, come on. No need to be so distant," Bullet whined. "I was with Jessie and Issac at the shooting range when I heard you were also here training. Since we got paired up to work on a contract, I thought we could chat for a bit."

Leon groaned in disgust. "Y'know 'Jessie' and 'Issac' are guns, right?" he quipped. "You don't have to go giving your guns people names and treat them like spoiled puppies."

Bullet laughed.

"Why wouldn't I name my precious little darlings?" she chimed.

"Right. Sometimes I forget that your brain's a few bullets short of a full reload," Leon thought aloud in frustrated annoyance. "That's my own fault."

Bullet's lips contorted into an amused smirk, despite Leon's blatant animosity towards her.

"Even with all of your venom and bile, I'm still looking forward to working another contract with you, Raven. You always know how to show a girl a good time," she said.

Bullet lightly scratched at her throat.

"The sight of a bullet or knife piercing flesh... The light leaving somebody's eyes... The look of terror on their face during their final moments... Killing is just such a rush!" she moaned.

Her cheeks blushed a shade red that was almost as vibrant as her lipstick as she gave Leon an almost intoxicated grin.

"And you do it better than anyone else."

Leon cringed, recoiling in revulsion. "Ugh! You are fucking unwell!" he snapped.

Leon had worked with a variety of other assassins, handlers, and intelligence agents during his time fulfilling contracts for Oblivion. The majority of them were sociopaths with an amount of morality that could be easily measured with a teaspoon… And then there was Bullet, the Oblivion agent he hated more than anyone else, no contest. From what Leon had heard through the rumor mill, Bullet's past was a mystery, and even Viper was unable to confirm basic information about her, such as her real name. The only concrete intel that everyone knew for sure about this deranged woman was that she was an expert marksman, and she got off to murder and death to a point where even seasoned professionals who had been with the organization for almost a decade found it off-putting. In a lot of ways, Bullet was worse than your typical scumbag assassin. She was a blood thirsty beast who needed to be kept on a chain or put down.

"Unless it has something to do with our next contract, just stay the hell away from me," Leon urged.

"Aw, you're so mean," Bullet sarcastically whined in a mocking baby voice.

She shrugged.

"Whatever. As long as I get to see you in action, I'm happy either way. Besides…"

The psychotic sniper winked at Leon.

"I love it when you play hard to get."

Leon clenched his fists, his irritation reaching a fever pitch to a point that it started to leave a sour taste in his mouth.

"Unless you want me to shank a knife between your ribs, cut it out with the sultry femme fatale bullshit and piss off…" he threatened in a cold, raspy growl.

Bullet smirked.

"Heh, don't go threatening me with a good time, babe," she teased. "But alright. I'll leave you be for now."

Bullet leaned forward, winking at Leon and blowing him a kiss.

"Until next time, darling," she chimed.

With that, Bullet walked away, finally giving Leon enough peace and quiet to ease the stress-induced tension headache that had begun grinding into the temples of his skull. His next contract couldn't come fast enough. The sooner he could get it done and over with, the sooner he could shake off the Oblivion poster girl for sexual harassment in the workplace.

Leon groaned, checking his watch.

"That time already? I still have to go to the grocery store to pick up ingredients for Jamie's bake sale," he muttered to himself. " Once again, there's no rest for the weary…"

***

Later that evening, after having made a detour to the supermarket, Leon returned home and started preparing for Jamie's bake sale. He decided to go simple, flavor-wise, and make vanilla bean cupcakes with strawberry buttercream. Leon precisely and meticulously measured his dry ingredients before setting them aside. He had bought a standing mixer almost a year ago as a treat to himself that he tragically never got much time to use, which was currently beating a mixture of butter, eggs, and sugar.

He knew he was going overboard for a high school bake sale, and that most of the donated items would probably be made from cake mix or smothered in store-bought frosting. In truth, baking was Leon's real passion. His mother owned a bakery, and some of his fondest memories were when he helped her make cakes at her shop. In another life, he would have gone to pastry school and opened a bakery. Unfortunately, the Black

Bird of Death gave up on that dream long before he joined Oblivion.

Once Leon had finished mixing all of the dry ingredients into the cake batter and the oven had finished preheating, he carefully poured the mixture into a pastry bag. Leon delicately piped the batter into each liner in the cupcake pan, his mind drifting down memory lane as he did.

The training his father put him through was extensive and brutal. Close-quarter combat, endurance training, knife throwing, and stealth training were just the tip of the iceberg. There was even one time when he was young, when Leon's dad had him throw knives at a target, and wouldn't let him take a break until he hit the mark blade-first twice in a row. Even after all the years that had passed since then, Leon could still perfectly picture how his hands bled that day, throwing knives one after another without cease until his father was ultimately satisfied with his form. Another memory Leon vividly recalled was when he was eight years old and holed himself up in his bedroom after yet another brutal training session with his father the day before.

There was a knock on his bedroom door.

"Leon, I'm coming in," his mother announced through the door.

Lydia Graves was a kind and gentle woman. She had dark brown hair, and both Leon and Lily had inherited her piercing, bright green eyes. She gently sat beside Leon, who still stared out in space, clenching his knees without even acknowledging her presence.

"Are you okay, Leon?" she asked.

Leon briefly looked up at her before turning away.

"Talking about it might make you feel better."

Leon bit his lip, clenching his knees even harder.

"You can tell me anything, Leon," she assured. "I promise I won't get mad."

Leon whimpered, finally relenting to his mother's gentle probing.

"...Does dad hate me?" he asked.

Lydia gave her son a gentle smile.

"Of course not. He loves you very much," she replied.

"He doesn't act like it..." Leon muttered glumly. "Why else would he make me train all the time?"

Leon's eyes started to tear up.

"I don't want to hurt anyone! I don't want to do it anymore! I just—" he choked, desperately trying not to cry.

Lydia wrapped Leon in a warm hug, gently stroking the back of his head.

"There, there," she whispered gently. "Let it all out."

Leon couldn't contain it anymore. He started wailing into his mother's arms. Lydia hugged him and stroked the back of his head, holding him tightly and not letting go. After a few minutes, Leon's crying slowly spluttered into a few tears and sniffles.

"I'm sorry," Lydia said. "Your dad— He has reasons, but I do wish he'd be more gentle with you."

Leon let out a small hiccup. Lydia gently wiped the tears from his eyes.

"He just wants to make sure that if it comes down to it someday, you can protect Lily and Jamie. You're their big brother. They'll depend on you to look out for them."

"Really?" Leon asked between his light sobs.

"Really," Lydia assured. "Families look out for each other. They protect and support one another."

Lydia kissed Leon on the forehead.

"I'll talk to your dad about going easier on you," she said.

Leon wiped his eyes, stifling his tears in a childish attempt to look tough.

"Okay," he replied. "Thanks…"

Lydia gently smiled at Leon once more.

"I was going to bake some cupcakes for after dinner today, and I could use a good helper," she said. "Would you like to help me?"

Leon lit up with excitement.

"Yeah!" he cheered.

Not long after that heart-to-heart with his mom, Leon's dad had eased up on him, at least a little bit. Two years later, however, his father disappeared. There was no warning or preamble. He simply left one day and never came back. Lily and Jamie were too young to truly remember him, let alone the hell he had put their big brother through. Leon never knew for sure why his dad had pushed him as hard as he did, or why he had up and walked out on the family out of the blue. Regardless of his reasons, Leon resented him for it. After all, what kind of respectable father would teach his young son how to kill?

Chapter 4

Early the next morning, Leon had been summoned back to The Final Exit by Viper. Bullet was already inside when Leon arrived, sitting at a table, polishing a sniper rifle while Viper read a newspaper behind the counter.

"If you're here, we're probably setting for our contract soon," Bullet thought aloud. "It's about time, honestly."

She gently stroked her rifle, as if it were a fluffy cat sitting on her lap.

"Lil Oscar here has been hankering for some fun."

"It's too early in the morning for your bullshit..." Leon grumbled, sitting down at the counter.

"Somebody's not a morning person," Bullet teased. "Here I thought I you couldn't get any grumpier."

Leon moaned before clenching his jaw in frustration. "Can we just get this over with?" he urged.

"You're always such a ray of sunshine, Raven," Viper chimed with deadpan sarcasm.

Viper neatly folded up his newspaper and set it down on the counter, clearing his throat as he prepared to speak.

"As you both know, the next contract concerns defectors who have banded together after severing ties with Oblivion," he explained. "Your primary target is a former Oblivion intelligence agent, code-named Charon, legal name Lorenzo James. Charon and his group settled in an area called Everitt, forty miles from here. It was once an old mining town that suffered hard times after an accident caused the coal mines to collapse, leaving them completely inoperable. Since then, the town has gone bankrupt and was officially declared unincorporated territory five years ago."

Viper's eyes darted back and forth between Leon and Bullet to make sure they were both paying attention.

"The operation for this contract will begin precisely at 9:45 PM this evening. Both of you will be deployed two miles out to avoid alerting them prematurely of your presence."

Viper crossed his arms, his gaze addressing Bullet.

"Bullet, your task will be to pick off sentries and other nearby targets from a distance. There's an old water tower on the town's outer perimeter you'll be able to use to shoot them down from."

Bullet giggled. "Oscar and I will make sure anyone in our line of sight never again sees the light of day," she declared.

This time, Viper turned his gaze to Leon.

"Once Bullet sends them scrambling, Raven. Your job will be to infiltrate the town proper, track down and silence Charon, and eliminate any other stragglers during the chaos," he said.

Leon nodded in silent affirmation to Viper's instructions. After a brief pause, Viper's shoulders stiffened.

"Remember, this is a contract commissioned by Undertaker himself," he warned. "There's no room for error, and any failures will lead all our heads on a spike."

"You don't say?" Leon dryly quipped.

Viper glared at Leon.

"Can you at least try to take this a little seriously?" Viper moaned.

"Yeah, yeah," Leon scoffed back flippantly, "Failure isn't an option. The last thing anyone wants to do is to piss off Undertaker. You still need to relax a little more. Just be glad you're the only one who doesn't have to do any of the heavy lifting."

"He has a point, you know," Bullet said. "Don't go stressing too hard about sucking up to Undertaker. We're assassins. We're expendable. We're used as tools to kill, and we're tossed out the moment we're no longer needed. Just get the job done, and you live to see another day, easy as pie."

Bullet shot Viper a mocking grin.

"Stress is bad for the skin, y'know," she teased. "It'd be a tragedy if you ruined that pretty face of yours getting your panties in a bunch. Besides, killing is supposed to be fun!"

Viper angrily pursed his lips. Leon could clearly see the gears of his fellow oblivion agent's mind at work as he weighed the pros and cons of whether or not to chew both of his coworkers out for being so casual about the operation, or to move on entirely. Viper was usually the type to needle others, either for information or just because he felt like it. However, before a big operation such as this, he became tightly wound and hyper-focused on the most minute details out of fear of failure. So naturally, Leon savored these moments where the tables were turned, and he could give Viper a taste of his own medicine.

"Well, excuse me for taking the job seriously..." Viper groaned in exasperation.

He cleared his throat.

"Anyway. You both will be disembarking for Everitt at 6:15 tonight. You two will meet at the usual rendezvous point before setting out."

Viper flashed Bullet and Leon a stern look.

"Don't be late."

***

Leon returned home from his briefing later that morning, once again having the apartment to himself while Jamie and Lily attended classes. After slowly drinking two cups of crappy instant coffee to perk himself up, he proceeded to get changed so he could finish making the cupcakes he had promised Jamie for the bake sale. By the early afternoon, Leon began his work in earnest.

The cupcakes he made the day before were carefully stored in air air-tight plastic container for freshness, and now it was time to prepare the frosting. He had already settled on a fresh strawberry buttercream for the cupcakes, setting aside a bowl of organic, freshly rinsed strawberries he bought just for the occasion. This form of confection was simple enough to make for Leon. Buttercream was a frosting made from equal parts sugar and room temperature butter whipped to perfection, Leon choosing in this case to substitute the usual vanilla extract for a strawberry one instead.

As the stand mixer cranked away with the butter and sugar mixture, he prepared a cutting board and a knife, placing a few strawberries on the surface to cut off the tips before finely cubing them. As he held the knife in his hand, he shuddered for a moment as an image flashed in his mind's eye. The mental picture consisted of Corpses. Lots and lots of corpses. Each one was either brutally stabbed, had their throat slit, or was lying still on the ground with a thrown knife sticking out of a vital vein or artery. The intrusive thought sent a chill down his spine. He took a breath in, holding it for a moment, before slowly exhaling.

"Pull yourself together..." he muttered quietly to himself.

Leon carried on, finely chopping and cubing the strawberries a few at a time. As he went about his menial task, he did everything he could to not think about the voices of his past victims begging for their lives or the stench of blood that always lingered afterward. Even if the infamous Black Bird of Death ever did get the chance to leave Oblivion, would it even be possible for him to lead a peaceful life? After the things he had seen and the atrocities he had committed with his own two hands, Leon knew deep down that he'd never know peace for the rest of his miserable life.

The tired assassin switched off the mixer and took out the bowl. He then took a rubber spatula to gently fold the finally cubed fruit within the frosting. Once he was satisfied with the distribution within the mixture, he loaded the buttercream frosting into a pastry bag and delicately swirled it on the tops of fluffy vanilla bean cupcakes, one at a time. By the time Leon finished, he had two dozen golden yellow cupcakes with a dainty and puffy pink strawberry buttercream frosting that blanketed the baked goods like a heavy snow.

Leon had already set aside a cupcake for himself as a little reward for his hard work. He unfurled the cake's wrapper and excitedly took a bite. The sponge was light, fluffy, moist, and airy. The buttercream was rich and sweet, with subtle and gentle tartness brought on by the fresh strawberries, preventing the sugary profile from becoming too overpowering. He took another bite, his little sweet treat making him forget the horrific outside world that had so completely crushed him in both mind and spirit, if only for one small happy moment. It was utter bliss.

As Leon enjoyed his snack, the lock on the front door clicked. Jamie returned home through the open door, with Lily closely following behind. Jamie was greeted by the sight of his big brother grinning as happily as a little kid while snacking on sugary food, and he couldn't help but let out a warm and hearty laugh upon seeing it.

"I can't remember the last time I saw you smile like that!" Jamie cheered. "Remind me to find a girl who loves me like you love baking and sugar!"

Leon rolled his eyes. "You make it sound like I'm a stressed-out and irritable loner," he said with a dour pout.

"I mean... You are, aren't you?" Jamie jokingly asked.

Leon almost made a snippy retort, cutting himself as he realized he was just about to prove his brother's point

He let out an annoyed huff. "Yeah, yeah, I hear you..." Leon quietly groaned in defeat while taking a napkin to clean off his fingers.

Lily remained silent during Jamie and Leon's exchange, biting and pursing her lip several times as she tried to figure out how best to say what was on her mind.

"It's good that you guys got home around the same time, though," Leon said, finishing his cupcake, licking some stray buttercream from his fingers. "I'm really sorry about this, but I got picked for a late-night conference out of town at the last minute, and I'm going to be heading out later this evening. I won't be back until late tomorrow morning."

Lily wearily narrowed her eyes as she glanced away from Leon. "Okay..." she muttered in a subdued, bitter tone.

Jamie sighed. "Take it that means you're not gonna make it to my game again?" he asked.

Leon hesitated for a moment.

"Yeah..." he replied, unable to look Jamie in the eyes as he did. "I'm sorry."

Jamie leaned his back on the countertop, and while his smile didn't break, it carried the burden of a bitter melancholy.

"It's okay. I'm used to it," he said.

Jamie's words pained Leon as if they were a knife piercing his heart.

"Are you mad?" he asked.

Jamie shrugged his shoulders. "It is what it is," he said. "I know you'd rather be doing other things rather than working, and you only work as hard as you do to provide for Lily and me, but it still sucks sometimes. The last time I remember you making it to a game was when I was still a freshman. This isn't the first time you missed something because of your hectic work schedule, and it won't be the last. That's just how the cookie crumbles sometimes."

Jamie's acceptance of the situation stung Leon deeply. He would have actually preferred it if Jamie were outwardly bitter and angry with his miserable failure of a big brother, because his acceptance caused Leon a painful guilt that was similar to asphyxiation, the way it balled up and constricted the back of his throat. If given the choice between experiencing the guilty conscience caused by the resigned disappointment of his younger brother or getting shot in the arm with a gun, Leon would have most certainly picked the firearm.

***

After wishing Jamie good luck on his game and saying a quick farewell to both his siblings, Leon made for the rendezvous point for their escort to Everitt. He and Bullet sat in the back of a black SUV that was carefully worn to blend in and look inconspicuous. The lukewarm twilight bathed the country roads as the remainder of the sinking sun's orange glow tapered across the cloudy sky. They had been on the road for about two and a half hours at that point. Bullet was bored, crossing her legs and irritably tapping her finger against the car door as she watched the rural landscapes blur by.

"Our contract's really out in the sticks this time around," she thought aloud.

Leon sat broodingly, slouching in his seat and leaning against his elbow on the armrest.

"Our job is in an abandoned mining town, perfect for vanishing off the grid. What did you expect?" he replied bluntly.

They drove another mile in silence, Bullet growing more irritated with each passing moment until she finally shot Leon an annoyed side-eye glance.

"Would it kill you to at least try to make a little small talk?" she quipped.

Leon rolled his eyes. "Fine," he relented with an annoyed huff. "Our primary target. Do you know him?"

"Worked with him once or twice," Bullet replied. "He provided some ammo and coordinates, and I shot someone dead. He was quiet and unassuming. Dreadfully dull, really."

Her lips slowly formed into a wistful and amused smile.

"That's why it's kind of surprising that boring man had the balls to ditch Oblivion, let alone start a collective mutiny over it. If nothing else, he's got guts. I'll give him that."

"Wonder where the desire to go through with this came from," Leon thought aloud.

"Does it matter?" Bullet scoffed.

"I'm just curious," Leon said flatly. "Lots of people get started in this business because they need money and have nowhere else to go. It makes me wonder if some straw broke the camel's back."

The sound of the bumpy and uneven dirt roads underneath hummed outside the car.

"We've already been over this, Raven," Bullet replied. "We're assassins. It doesn't matter what our reasons are. We're tools meant to kill, and we're tossed out like old trash the moment we're no longer useful. Getting the job done is all that matters, Nothing else."

Leon stared out the car window as early evening stars started to twinkle in the night sky.

"And Oblivion essentially runs a monopoly on this industry," he said. "They have powerful financial backers and many influential allies in the halls of power. If you betray the organization, there's no escape. There's nowhere in the developed world you could run to where they couldn't hunt you down. Any person who rebels or leaves is a dead man. That's probably why Charon chose to band with some other defectors and hole up in the middle of a remote ghost town. Objectively speaking, it's the best shot he has at escaping."

As Leon spoke this truth aloud, he cursed his lot in life. His fate was sealed the moment he joined Oblivion. Whether he met his end at the hands of another assassin or kicked the bucket via some other grizzly outcome he had failed to consider, Oblivion would own him, body and soul, until the day he died. In Leon's eyes, Charon's rebellion was foolish. Pointless. It was always better to just bend to those with power than to stand up to them and be broken, especially if the people you cared about most would get caught in the crossfire. Yet even after acknowledging that truth, a small flame of envy burned within the Black Bird of Death, jealous that Charon was courageous enough to defy an authority that Leon himself had already obediently bent the knee to.

The car stopped.

"This is as far as I can take you," the handler in the driver's seat said. "Any closer, and we risk alerting the targets to our presence prematurely."

The handler, Bullet, and Leon got out of the car. Dusk had fallen, and the driver had pulled off to the side of an old dirt road that ran through a mountainous woodland. The handler followed Leon and Bullet as they retrieved their equipment from the trunk of the car.

The handler pointed off into the distance down the road. "Everitt is two miles that way," he said. "Stay out of sight, and make for your assigned positions."

The handler gave both Bullet and Leon an earpiece.

"When I give the green light, you two will begin the operation."

Chapter 5

Everitt. A small town in the countryside. Once a bustling settlement nestled in the mountains during the turn of the twentieth century, it was now a shambled set of ruins where Oblivion deserters hid themselves away. The old wooden buildings were decaying, and the only source of light was the makeshift torches and fires that various defectors used to light the way in the dark as they acted as lookouts for those who rested inside. The collective was an even mix of men and women, mostly former handlers and intelligence agents with a very small handful of low-level assassins. Even in the dead of night, an aura of tense restlessness could be felt in the area. It was a suppressed and unspoken fear that at any moment, agents from Oblivion could come to kill them all.

Off in the distance, about twenty feet away from the town's outer perimeter, Bullet scaled up the ladder of an old and empty water tower. When she reached the top, she set down her briefcase and started assembling her favorite rifle she lovingly referred to as Oscar. The stars shone brightly in the sky, embracing the waxing crescent moon that watched from above. As Bullet assembled her rifle, she took careful note of the direction the wind was blowing, knowing full well from experience that even the most minute details in the weather conditions and wind direction could mean the difference between landing and missing a shot.

Bullet attached a silencer to Oscar's muzzle and then finally secured and aligned the scope. She took note of the various areas sentries that patrolled Everitt, prioritizing those who were furthest away from places they could shelter and cover from gunfire. Her earpiece gave a quiet chirp.

"Status report," the handler said.

"I'm in position and awaiting further orders," Leon said through the earpiece

Bullet smiled with an excited crooked grin.

"I'm in position, locked and loaded," she said. "I'm ready to proceed whenever."

"Roger that," the handler buzzed in Bullet's ear. "Begin the operation."

Bullet licked her lips, the anticipation of the kill burning inside her at a fever pitch. Bullet locked in on her first target.

"It's showtime," she cooed, pulling the trigger.

***

Blood, skull fragments, and brain matter scattered as the first sentry was shot in the head. Just as the group realized what was happening, two more sentries were also shot in the head in quick succession, their bodies dropping to the ground as the pungent smell of iron polluted the air.

"We're under attack!" someone shouted.

"Alert Charon right now—" another sentry ordered, before being shot down mid-sentence

Leon observed from the shadows as the encampment was sent into utter disarray. Screams filled the air, the defectors scrambling for cover, desperately trying to figure out the sniper's location based on the direction of the gunfire.

A small beep chirped in Leon's ear.

"All clear, Raven." The handler reported through Leon's earpiece. "Commence your extermination. Leave no survivors."

"Roger that," Leon said, readying several knives.

Leon discreetly snuck up behind a nearby defector and slit his throat. Just as his comrades sensed something was amiss, Leon launched two knives into their necks, his query dropping to the ground and bleeding out in seconds. While others scrambled for shelter and met their ends failing to do so as Bullet's gunfire rained down upon them, Leon quickly and discreetly ended everyone who had managed to find cover. In the shroud of darkness, Leon gracefully maneuvered through the mayhem, his victims dropping like flies one after another, launching knives into vital arteries of his victims, stabbing them from behind, or mercilessly slitting their throats.

The resistance group was no match for Leon and Bullet's combined assault. Bullet sent them scrambling with gunfire, and Leon was a phantom of death that slipped in during the chaos. The defectors did their best to fight back, each one resisting until their very last breath, but it was no use. In the industry of murder-for-hire, each defector was a mere small fry. A footnote barely anyone knew existed. While they were anonymous grunts, Leon and Bullet were two of the best assassins that Oblivion had to offer. With such a great gap in skill, calling the ongoing onslaught "a battle" would have been a blatant lie. The truthful and much more accurate term for the whole affair would have been "slaughter".

"I'll fucking kill you!" a woman roared in fury, charging at Leon with a lead pipe.

Leon remained unfazed, readying a knife and throwing in the same quick fluid motion. The knife impaled her right eye and pierced her brain. She fell to the ground, her scream echoing for only a moment before it was silenced entirely. Leon unceremoniously plucked the knife from her skull, dripping the excess blood and brain matter as if it were acrylic paint from a brush. The Black Bird of Death gave a weary sigh, cracking his neck and stretching out his left shoulder. He then proceeded to continue his hunt, leaving a sea of corpses in his wake.

***

In a matter of minutes, the screams and sounds of bloodshed rapidly dwindled until you could only hear the rustling of trees in the wind. Bodies littered the ghost town inside and out as pools of blood saturated the soil. Leon surveyed the carnage, unharmed and barely breaking a sweat. A gentle breeze carried the pungent scent of iron to his nose and lips. He always hated this putrid odor, and the current sight of the massacre before him made him feel broken and hollow. He loosened the tie around his neck and adjusted his shirt collar before he checked his watch.

"We're making good time at least," Leon muttered to himself. "Charon's still unaccounted for, though."

At that moment, Leon's ears picked up the slightest sound of wood floorboards creaking under a footstep. With a rapid turn of his heel, he threw a knife at the source.

"Shit!" Charon cursed, the knife knocking his pistol out of his hands.

Charon sprinted away into the nearby thicket, scrambling as he almost tripped over a tree root and had his face scratched by low-hanging tree branches. Charon kept running and running—

"FUCK!" he screamed, falling over onto the ground, a sharp pain shooting through the back of his thigh. He sat up, clenching his leg in pain, hunched over, and wincing at the sight of a knife handle that pierced his flesh. Leon emerged from the shadows, another knife in hand, ready to finish the job.

"You..." Charon snarled in contempt. "You're the Black Bird of Death."

"I am," Leon replied flatly. "I was asked by Undertaker himself to kill you and the other agents who left their posts at Oblivion. Sorry, but orders are orders."

Charon gritted his teeth, staring daggers at Leon.

"Well, what are you waiting for?" he barked. "Just kill me already, you son of a bitch!"

Leon held his knife steady in his hand. He bit his lip, his curiosity getting the better of him

"Tell me... Why try to defect from Oblivion?" he asked.

Charon growled. "Because I didn't want any part of this dirty business anymore!" he replied.

Despite Leon's straight face, his primary target's explanation left him puzzled and baffled.

"That's it? You were prepared to disappear and live off the grid entirely simply to have a chance to escape Oblivion's grasp, all because you simply wanted out?"

"I only joined Oblivion because I needed money!" Charon spat. "My daughter was diagnosed with cancer, and I couldn't afford her treatments!"

His eyes began to tear up from both the overwhelming weight of his righteous fury and his utter despair brought on by fate's senseless cruelty. He tightly clenched his fist, punching it into the ground with a violent force.

"And then she died while I was on an assignment! I'm a crappy dad who couldn't even be there for his little girl's final moments! But everything I've done, every terrible thing I took part in... I did it for her, dammit!"

Leon grimaced, understanding Charon's anguish all too well. He knew if something ever happened to Lily or Jamie, and everything he sacrificed to Oblivion was rendered meaningless, he would've cursed his fate like a forsaken sinner raging against the heavens.

"She was my only reason for living!" Charon cried. "No matter what I do! I'm a dead man! If I tried to carry on with this unforgivable line of work, I was going to kill myself! If I tried to leave, Oblivion was going to kill me!"

There was a raging fire that burned passionately in his eyes.

"So to hell with it! If Oblivion is going to kill me one way or another, I want to live and die on my terms! Not theirs!"

He tilted his head, looking upon Leon as if he were a foul creature who was even lower than the absolute scum of the earth.

"But you wouldn't understand! You're just another heartless killing machine like the rest of them!"

Charon huffed slowly and heavily. "So what are you waiting for?" he growled. "Just kill me already—"

BANG!

A gunshot echoed in the wilderness. Charon's body fell to the ground with a thud as fragments of his skull and brain smeared against the bases of the trees behind him. Leon looked behind his shoulder and saw Bullet standing nearby, holding a handgun and brandishing an annoyed scowl.

"Ugh... I can't stand men who go too ham on foreplay..." she complained while placing her firearm in a holster at her waist.

Leon lowered his knife and said nothing. Bullet approached him slowly, staring coldly into his eyes.

SMACK!

Without hesitation, Bullet slapped Leon across the face. He recoiled as the pain stung and radiated across his left cheek.

"Are you stupid or something?" Bullet asked, her voice dropping to a deep and cold, husky contralto. "What the hell is wrong with you?"

Leon winced, flustered and thrown off by both Bullet's reprimanding questions and sudden strike.

"I..." Leon stammered, his words failing him.

"Hesitation like that is liable to get you killed and potentially ruin an entire operation!" Bullet hissed in icy fury. "It doesn't matter what the reason is. If you get paid to kill someone, you kill them! End of story!"

Bullet quietly grunted in frustration.

"What a libido killer…" she grumbled to herself in disappointment. "All that build up, and you couldn't even finish."

"Bullet, I—" Leon stuttered.

"Not another word from you, Raven," Bullet ordered. "We finished the job, and that's what matters. Out of respect for your past work, I'll keep my mouth shut about your screw up."

She turned up her nose in disgust at Leon.

"But for fuck's sake! Pull yourself together!"

Chapter 6

When Leon was ten years old, he had a conversation with his father on the front porch of his childhood home. It was a still, quiet summer night. The air was humid and muggy as July fireflies scattered across the front lawn. Leon sat on the front step while his father sat in a foldout lawn chair nursing a glass of cheap bourbon on the rocks.

Marshal Graves was an intimidating man. He had disheveled and shortly trimmed dark red hair and dead hazel eyes, with heavy shadows brooding under them. Mild stubble ran across his cheeks and jawline, his face worn in a way that the wrinkles it bore made his resting expression resemble a disappointed glare. Marshal exuded the aura of a shell-shocked retired soldier who could still kill at a moment's notice if the situation called for it. No matter how much he puzzled over it, Leon could never fathom what his mother saw in the man.

As a young boy, Leon stared out at the fireflies that dazzled their front yard. Marshal set his drink on the ground, grappling with the right words to say to his son.

"Your form's improved the past few days…" he said in a stiff and awkward tone.

Leon remained quiet, not even acknowledging his father's presence.

"Er… Um… Do you like those lightning bugs?"

Leon did not answer. Marshal always struggled when it came to interacting with his son. Handling a knife, close-quarter combat, that was easy. Being a father and trying to relate to his oldest son… That was another matter entirely. It wasn't so much that Marshal didn't want to be a good dad to his children— it was more so that he had no idea how.

"You know, your accuracy with knife throwing has improved a lot, too," Marshal said, forcing a friendly grin. "I remember when you started, you couldn't even hit water standing in a boat."

Leon glumly stared down at his feet.

"...I hate it," he said meekly. "I hate the training you put me through. I don't want to fight. I don't want to hurt anyone."

Marshal gave a weary sigh, unsure of whether he was concerned about his son's potential weakness or proud that he had retained his mother's kindness despite the failings of his father.

"No good person does," he replied.

Leon gritted his teeth as tears started streaming down his face.

"Then why make me do it!?" he angrily cried.

Marshal got up from his seat, sitting on the front stoop beside his son, and gently placed his hand on Leon's shoulder

"There will come a day when I won't be around anymore," he said, staring up at the stars in the sky. "I want to make sure you can protect yourself, and the things you care about most."

Leon looked up at his father's face, noticing for the first time in his life the broken man that hid behind his tough exterior.

"What do you mean?" he asked.

"Things change, Leon," his father replied. "Nothing lasts forever."

A pained and melancholy smile carved itself into Marshal's lips as he gazed upon the moon.

"I know I'm terrible at showing it, but I love you, Lily, Jamie, and your mom very much," he said. "That's why, if something ever happens to me and your mom, I want you to be able to be there for Lily and Jamie, Leon. They'll be all you ever have. They will need their big brother to watch out for them— to protect them from anyone who would want to hurt them."

That was the last conversation Leon ever had with his dad. The next day, the man known as Marshal Graves disappeared without a trace and never came back. No matter how much time passed, no matter how much Leon was able to rationalize the reasoning for the hellish training his father put him through, no matter how much he tried to choke it down and feel nothing, he could never let go of the bitter resentment he had for the man.

***

Leon had returned home from the Oblivion operation by four in the morning. The entire affair left a sour taste in Leon's mouth, and he didn't even bother to attempt to sleep when he got back. Instead, he chipped away at a cheap bottle of bourbon, like he always did when a job left him shaken up. After a glass of booze, brooding and stewing in the shame of his failures, Leon finished his bourbon and went to take a shower. When he got out, he changed into a pair of sweat pants and an old, plain white T-shirt, switching out his alcoholic beverage for a cup of coffee now that a new day had begrudgingly begun.

Thankfully, after a job of that scale, the handler that accompanied them had instructed Leon and Bullet to take the rest of the weekend off to rest and recuperate. That said, the only activity that currently sounded remotely appealing to the Black Bird of Death was dissociating while staring at a blank wall. By nine in the morning, Lily had emerged from her bedroom, letting out a small yawn. As she entered the kitchen in her bright pink pajamas, she was startled by the sight of her big brother lost in thought and drowning in his own angst at the kitchen island.

"Please tell me you slept last night..." she said in an exasperated moan.

Leon shrugged his shoulders. "You hate it when I lie to you," he muttered back.

Lily pulled up a stool and sat across from Leon. "What happened?" she asked.

"I don't want to get into it, but the conference last night got pretty rough," Leon explained. "It was total chaos, I fucked up at one point, and got a nasty earful from one of my coworkers because of it."

"If it makes you feel any better, the cupcakes you made for Jamie's bake sale yesterday were really popular," Lily said. "All of them sold out in minutes, and a bunch of moms were raving about how pretty, perfect, and delicious they were."

Lily gave out a small laugh.

"They were pretty surprised that it was my workaholic big brother who made them, and not me."

Leon grinned weakly at his sister. "That does make me feel a little better," he relented.

Lily bit her lip. "It's not too late, y'know..." she said.

Leon's weak, happy expression shifted to a fatigued and defeated frown upon hearing his sister's words.

"You hate what you do for a living, Leon, I know it. It's always been your dream to open a bakery. We have some money saved up now, and Jamie and I aren't helpless kids anymore."

Leon gave a quiet and defeated exhale from his mouth.

"We've been over this again and again, Lily," he said in a glum and lethargic tone. "I want you and Jamie to focus on your studies so you can get a good job and make an honest living. I want you both to be okay in case something ever happens to me."

Leon slouched in his seat, giving Lily a warm and bright smile that didn't reach his eyes.

"Besides. I'm okay. I don't need that dream anymore…"

Lily hesitated, wanting so badly to try and reach out to her brother once more. In the end, she sulked in defeat, knowing full well that there was no way to get through to her older sibling while he was in such a stubborn emotional state.

"If you say so…' she said, while standing up. "Anyway, I got a group project I gotta work on at the campus library today, so I should get washed up and get going."

"It's fine," Leon replied. "Keep up the good work."

As Lily walked away, she took a moment halfway to her room to look back at her brother.

"Promise me you won't push yourself too hard, okay?" she said

"I promise," Leon replied, painfully self-aware that he was making a promise he couldn't keep.

Leon understood perfectly how Lily felt, but all the same, there was no going back to living a happy, normal life for him. Even if by some divine miracle manifested by a god in a machine that Oblivion ceased to be and left him free to do whatever he wanted with his life, he was too far gone. Nothing would change the fact that Leon Graves was a killer with a body count he lost track of long, long ago. He was beyond saving, and while he couldn't confess the truth to his sister out loud, Leon knew deep down his dream of opening a bakery died the same day their mother did.

***

Later that afternoon, Jamie took Leon out to the local shopping mall, insisting that he should take his older brother out for some fun as a way to thank him for helping out with the bake sale despite his busy schedule. Having all but dragged him by the arm, Jamie took him through several storefronts and, against all odds, even persuaded him to play a round of mini-golf. Leon tried his best to feign interest, but was otherwise just going through the motions, and it showed.

Every time Jamie tried to talk to Leon, his responses were terse and to the point, or at least more so than usual. From the corner of his eye, Jamie occasionally spotted Leon letting out a deep sigh or staring off into the distance when he thought no one was looking. They had sat down for a quick lunch in the mall food court, with Leon barely touching his food. Jamie stepped away to buy a soft pretzel.

Leon leaned back in his chair, taking a breath in and letting out a slow and heavy sigh. The faint ambient sound of chatter was overwhelming. The sight of families having lunch together, high schoolers loudly laughing together as they walked by, and everyday people going about their day, blissfully unaware that they were in the same room as a deadly killer... It made his stomach churn.

"But you wouldn't understand! You're just another heartless killing machine like the rest of them!"

Charon's words from the night before echoed over and over again in Leon's head. No matter what he did, no matter whatever else he tried to think about, the Black Bird of Death could only hyper-fixate on the fact that he was indeed a heartless killing machine. Leon's spine stiffened, his face going blank. Flashes of various assassinations he committed blurred in his mind's eye.

"You're just another heartless killing machine like the rest of them!"

Leon gulped. The more he tried to think of absolutely anything else, the more his despair snowballed out of control. What right did he have to live on like this? Like nothing ever happened... How could he just carry on as if he didn't spend the previous night slaughtering a group of people for his own financial gain?

"You're just another heartless killing machine like the rest of them!"

His heart raced. The corners of his vision darkened as the walls started to close in around him. Leon's face didn't convey a single emotion, but he couldn't breathe. He was a terrible person, he was a murderer, he didn't deserve to be alive, he—

"Leon?" a voice called.

Jamie stood beside Leon, holding a soft pretzel in each hand, his visible look of concern slowly pulling his older brother back to reality.

"You good?" he asked.

Leon was still in a slight daze. It took him a short moment before he could successfully compartmentalize his self-loathing once more, putting on a straight face to respond to Jamie's question.

"I'm fine," he replied flatly.

Jamie gave him a pensive look before holding one of the soft pretzels out to Leon. "Here, I got you one too," he said in a timid mutter.

He gave Leon a weak smile as he handed him the salty and greasy mall pastry by the napkin

"Thanks," Leon said.

Jamie sat down across from him once again, taking a bite of his pretzel and swallowing it.

"I'm sorry for dragging you around like this," he said sheepishly. "I overheard you talking with Lily earlier this morning and... I just wanted to cheer you up."

Leon frowned. "How much did you hear?" he asked.

"Everything," Jamie answered with a weary exhale. "You're not as good at lying as you think you are, man."

"I see..." Leon gloomily muttered back.

Jamie laid his napkin on the table before placing his soft-pretzel on top of it.

"I know I'm just your kid brother, but Lily and I worry about you," he explained. "I understand that it's complicated, and there's probably a reason why you haven't stepped away from whatever it is that you do for a living, or never really opened up about it to either of us. That said, the way you're so hellbent on supporting us, and watching you shoulder everything all by yourself— it hurts Lily and me more than you can imagine."

Jamie's eyes were glassy, his usual friendly grin tinted with melancholy and nostalgia.

"I honestly can't remember what our dad even looks like," he confessed. "Whenever I try to picture any sort of father figure in my life... You're the only person that ever comes to mind."

Jamie placed his hand on Leon's shoulder.

"You've done so much for Lily and me, and we want to be there for you, too. So maybe at least try to meet us halfway, okay? Believe it or not, we love you, and we don't want to see you get hurt because of us."

Jamie's honesty reminded Leon of the summer sun. It was warm. Bright. Radiant to a point where it was nearly blinding. It was an emotional punch to the gut, the way he envied this trait in his little brother. All the Black Bird of Death knew was self-reliance, deceit, violence, and killing. Such straightforward compassion was something that never came naturally to him, nor was it something he ever had the luxury of having. As he had experienced firsthand, many times before, most problems in life couldn't be solved by simply being true to yourself. Most of the time, all anyone could ever do was choke down all the bitter unfairness and injustice in the world and carry on suffering in silence. The real world didn't give a shit if you were dying inside or barely keeping it together. It unceremoniously moved on, with or without you.

"I'll try," Leon answered, once again knowing full well he was making yet another promise he couldn't keep.

Chapter 7

When Leon was nineteen years old, he was working a part-time job as a dishwasher. It was one of three part-time jobs he had, in fact, also working construction during the day, and as a paid-for-hire day laborer with whatever time he had left spare. It had been a year since his mother died, almost to the day. She used to own a bakery, and she clung to it even harder after his dad walked out on the family. When the economy hit some rough times, she did everything she could to keep it open, but in the end, it was all for nothing.

Lydia Graves worked herself into the ground trying to both keep her business open and provide for her children. Even with Leon picking up the slack to care for his younger siblings, Lydia was simply one woman trying to achieve the impossible. She literally worked herself to death. When all was said and done, Lydia was dead, her business went bankrupt anyway, she left behind her three children with nothing, and now they were forced to fend for themselves.

Leon exited the back door of the bar where he worked and into the back alleyway, with two large trash bags filled to the brim and slung over his shoulders. As the cold night caressed his skin, Leon couldn't recall if he even had gotten a chance to sit down that day. He was tired; his feet were killing him, and the only reason he was able to keep going at all was for his brother and sister. Even after they sold their childhood home, money was tight, and the last thing he wanted was for Lily and Jamie to end up in foster care.

That month's rent was five days past due, and what little savings he did have were decimated by having to take Jamie to the doctor for strep throat and a sinus infection. By that point in time, Leon was becoming more and more afraid that both he and his younger siblings would be going hungry if he didn't figure something out soon.

With a heavy huff, Leon flung the trash bags into the alleyway dumpster. He was overwhelmed and barely holding it together, desperately trying to focus on finishing his current shift before he tackled every other problem and responsibility actively crushing him beneath their weight.

"Good evening," a voice greeted.

Leon jumped, startled by the sight of a slender man, who was probably only a year or two older than he was, standing behind him. The stranger had neatly trimmed blonde hair and a pretty face, wearing a simple brown cardigan over a black shirt, with a gray backpack suspended from his shoulders. The stranger had an almost angelic beauty, but gave off a slimy vibe that Leon didn't like one bit.

"Sorry. I didn't mean to startle you," he said. "I was just looking for someone."

The man gave Leon a friendly grin.

"Are you perchance Leon Graves, son of Marshal Graves?" he asked.

Leon didn't say a word, only giving a cold glare to the man. The man laughed in response.

"You're not one for a poker face!" he teased. "That look of contempt gives me all the confirmation I need."

Leon rolled his eyes. "What do you want, smartass?" he asked curtly.

"Just a moment of your time," the man said. "I was hoping we could chat for a moment."

"I got bills to pay," Leon replied. "If you're here just to yap, then piss off. They'll fire me if I take too long—"

"Alright, then, I'll make it worth your while," the man interrupted.

The man placed his backpack on the ground, unzipping it and pulling out three high-quality throwing knives and a large wad of cash.

"Let's play a short lil game," he chimed.

The man pointed towards a medium-sized wooden crate that was discarded about fifteen feet further down the alley.

"For every knife you land blade-first into that box, I'll give you one hundred dollars," he said. "Land all three, and I'll give you another two hundred dollars as a bonus."

Leon looked the suspicious stranger up and down. Contrary to his charming facade, Leon noticed that, despite the man's friendly expression, his eyes were cold and shifty, as if he were constantly evaluating everyone and everything around him. Whoever he was, he came prepared for a sales pitch and seemed to have done a great deal of research beforehand. Considering how he had already mentioned his deadbeat of a dad, and then created a challenge centered around throwing knives, Leon could only conclude that this stranger's motivations and affiliations were morally questionable at their absolute best. Still, five hundred dollars was more than a week's pay from one of his part-time jobs, and he wasn't about to wipe his ass with the chance to make some easy money.

"Fine," Leon grumbled back.

"Marvelous," the man cheered. "Then let's get started."

The man handed Leon the throwing knives, and Leon took them all by the handle. It had been almost a decade since he held a knife in his hand in such a manner, but the muscle memory remained. It was the same sensation a *normal* person would equate with never forgetting how to ride a bike. Leon steadied his breath, holding out one of the knives as he gauged the distance and angle between himself and his target. Finally, in a fluid and seamless motion, Leon threw each knife at the wooden crate in rapid succession. Each one rhythmically landed blade-first into the crate with pinpoint precision and accuracy. The stranger slowly clapped his hands in applause, the sound practically pedantic.

"Well done!" he coyly cheered.

He handed Leon five hundred dollars from the large wad of bills he had brought with him, and as far as Leon could tell at a glance, each dollar was real, non-counterfeit currency that could be used as cold, hard cash.

"If you don't mind getting your hands a little dirty, how would you like another chance to earn even more easy money?" he asked.

Leon didn't answer, instead opting to coldly stare the suspicious stranger down once again.

"I understand your apprehension. After all, I'm just a shady rando who startled you in a dark alleyway," the man said. "But your skills are being wasted on such pointless menial labor."

The stranger pulled out a business card from his sleeve with a dramatic flourish.

"Why not at least take some time to think about it? If you end up taking interest in this generous offer, just show up at the address on this card. When you arrive, just tell whoever's working behind the counter that 'Viper' sent you there."

Viper turned his back to Leon, walking away and playfully waving goodbye as he disappeared into the night.

"Until we meet again!" he called.

Leon sighed, flipping over the card in his hand.

"The Final Exit," he quietly read aloud.

Leon shook his head in annoyance.

"Now what kind of mess did I just get myself into…"

***

Earlier that morning, Leon had been summoned to The Final Exit to meet with Undertaker. Once again, it seemed there was no rest for the weary. The last operation left a sour taste in Leon's mouth, and the flavor was still bitter on his tongue over the remainder of the weekend. He sat at the front counter brooding, as he always did when he awaited a new contract or intelligence briefing. Viper brewed a fresh pot of coffee, the premium beans he used smelling heavenly as the aroma swirled in the air. Were it not for the fact that the roast was being prepared by an assassin whose favorite pastime was concocting poison, Leon would have considered asking for a cup.

Viper playfully leaned on the counter, directing a seemingly easy-going grin that yet again didn't meet his eyes towards Leon.

"How'd your last assignment go?" he asked.

"I see you're back to your usual annoying self," Leon quipped while rolling his eyes.

"What do you mean?" Viper replied. "I'm the same as I always am. "

Leon wasn't sure why, but for some reason, he found Viper's usual antics even more insufferable than usual.

"Ugh, you're like some annoying rich kid…" he groaned. "You act all high and mighty, poking and probing everyone else when times are good, but you become a stressed-out and annoyed hot mess whenever something might not go your way."

Viper shrugged his shoulders. "I have no idea what you're talking about," he scoffed.

"Sure you don't," Leon replied with a pointed and sarcastic bite.

Leon stood up from his stool, stretching out his left arm and cracking his elbow.

"Anyway…" Viper trailed off, changing the subject. "Considering you and Bullet came back in one piece, and Oblivion hasn't taken a hit out on any of us, it's safe to assume the job went without a hitch, yeah?"

"Yeah," Leon replied flatly.

Viper's eyes narrowed, his gaze prodding Leon like the needle of a syringe.

"I heard Bullet was in quite the mood after the job, though," he said. "Any idea what might've pissed her off this time around?"

"Knowing Bullet, it could be a great many things, so who's to say?" Leon dryly mused. "You're more than welcome to ask her yourself."

"Ha! Talk to that crazy bitch? Hard pass!" Viper playfully chimed.

"For once, you and I agree on something," Leon moaned.

Leon gave a short weary yawn.

"Out of morbid curiosity, Viper. Have you ever thought about what you would be doing if you had never become an assassin?" he asked.

Viper gave Leon an annoyed pout. "What kind of question is that?" he replied mockingly.

"Humor me," Leon lethargically insisted.

Viper crossed his arms. "No such thoughts have ever crossed my mind," he confessed. "Let's just say, for me, killing with poison is considered a bit of a family tradition. Studying, concocting, and killing with poison was what I was made to do."

"So, where did the intelligence gathering factor into that?" Leon asked.

"Oblivion runs a monopoly on murder-for-hire, and I'm not suited for direct combat," Viper explained. "Intelligence gathering and dealing is the primary way I can assist with Oblivion contracts without having to go out in the field as much. I primarily joined Oblivion to schmooze big shots like Undertaker on behalf of someone else. Otherwise, I'm no different than you and Bullet."

Leon frowned. "Rewarded for getting the job done, and then tossed aside when you're no longer useful," he glumly thought aloud once more. "Sounds about right."

"That's just how the cookie crumbles," Viper said. "Intelligence is the primary way I can remain in good standing when my poison expertise is not needed. As long as I stay Undertaker's good side, and provide results, that's all that matters."

Viper dropped his usual rehearsed smile, revealing an apathetic and bitter resignation.

"In the end, it's always better to bend over backward to please those who have power so they don't use it to crush you. That's just how the world works. There's no point in questioning it."

***

It wasn't long after their chat that Undertaker arrived. After he dismissed Viper, he sat down at a table across from Leon. Undertaker's assistant, Styx, having finished preparing a cappuccino for her master, stood behind him at the ready until given her next order.

"You and Bullet did well exterminating those rats," Undertaker commended.

Leon nodded in obedient affirmation. "Thank you, sir," he replied.

Undertaker pulled out a large envelope from an inner pocket of his bespoke suit jacket.

"Your share of the commission," he said, pushing the envelope across the table.

"Thank you, sir," Leon said as he graciously took his payment.

Undertaker picked up his mug, taking a small sip of his cappuccino and savoring the aroma.

"Now for your next contract," he said while gently placing the mug back on the table. "Ordinarily, I would prefer not to assign missions so close to one another, but this next operation is on a tight timetable and requires a high-caliber assassin with your specific skillset."

Undertaker's eyes darted towards Styx before returning to Leon. Styx bowed in response to the subtle gesture before clearing her throat.

"Your client is an underground weapons dealer and manufacturer. As a result of a mutually beneficial agreement, Oblivion and this organization have enjoyed a profitable partnership," she explained. "However, our client has earned the ire of a meddlesome prosecutor. Both our groups benefit from allies in the halls of power who have agreed to turn a blind eye to our activities, either in exchange for a payoff or to avoid having some delicate information leaked to the general public."

"However, this self-righteous idiot refuses to play ball," Undertaker shrewdly added. "He's a family man with a strong sense of justice. It would be a massive inconvenience to Oblivion should his little crusade gain some momentum. So we'll force his hand into cooperating before he can become an issue."

"What do you mean?" Leon asked.

"This prosecutor has a wife and two children," Styx explained. "The client intends to send to message to this upstart that he has the capacity to destroy everything he holds dear. He has seen fit to take out a hit on his oldest child. An eight-year-old boy by the name of Charlie."

Leon's stomach hit the floor.

"This contract is to be completed before tomorrow morning, and only our best will do," Undertaker ordered. "The client requested that the job be handled by the Black Bird of Death specifically. Viper will apprise you of your mission briefing before you leave here today."

Leon bit his lip. "Sir…" he said. "If I may, I'm not sure if comfortable with assassinating a child. Surely there's another way to—"

"Are you questioning me?" Undertaker interjected, his eyes radiating a cold and icy fury.

Leon froze.

"You do recall our organization's policy regarding refusal of a contract, yes?" Undertaker asked.

Leon clenched his fists in his lap, unable to look Undertaker in the eye.

"I do, sir," he stuttered. "I just— I don't know if I can through killing—"

"Silence," Undertaker ordered.

Undertaker took another sip of cappuccino, the clank of the mug punctuating the intense quiet as he once again gently placed it back on the table.

"You know, Raven, I know you originally joined Oblivion to provide for your precious little brother and sister," he said. "If you wish to refuse a contract and forfeit your life, that's your decision. Yet are you not concerned for your family's safety? It would be an absolute shame if something were to happen to them."

Leon's eyes widened in wild and protective rage as he bolted upright from his seat.

"They have nothing to do with this!" he roared.

Styx moved to subdue Leon, but froze at the mere sight of Undertaker silently raising his hand as a signal for her to stop.

"But they have everything to do with the current situation," Undertaker said. "You are a valuable asset to Oblivion. You were requested specifically, and I will not risk offending such an important client."

Undertaker did not raise his voice, nor did his face betray even the faintest outward sign of anger regarding his subordinate's outburst. He used the same aloof and detached tone he'd use for any type of business deal. Despite that, his words were chilling and powerful.

"I'll lay it out nice and simple for you, Raven. Refuse or fail this contract, and I will end the lives of your precious family. Succeed, and I will reward you as I always do. Do you understand?"

Leon let out a shaky exhale. "Yes, sir," he trembled in defeat.

"Good," Undertaker said, while standing up.

Undertaker casually approached Leon, the way someone might approach a loved one for a friendly one-armed hug. However, the cold, icy fury that radiated from the CEO's eyes as it tensed his shoulders and fingers told a different story. Leon was all but holding his breath as Undertaker stared him down like a divine being casting judgment upon a mortal sinner. With absolutely no hesitation or remorse, Undertaker punched Leon in the stomach, just under his ribcage. The Black Bird of Death doubled over, coughing as he gasped for the air that was knocked out of his lungs.

"Know your place, whelp," Undertaker quietly spat. "Because of your prior accomplishments, I will overlook your insolence just this once. But should you disrespect me again, I will show you no mercy. You are to do as I say and obey without question. A pawn that does not listen to its master has no use to me."

Leon gasped, still struggling to regain his senses. Undertaker made for the door.

"Come, Styx. We have other places we must be," he ordered.

Styx silently nodded, stepping around Leon as if he were nothing more than a piece of furniture, and followed her master out the door. While Leon steadied his breathing, he fully fell to the floor with a vacant stare, utterly crushed by the ever-growing weight of the burdens he carried.

Chapter 8

Later that afternoon, Leon attempted to go through his usual routine regimen at an Oblivion Training Facility. After his brutal meeting with Undertaker, he had his mission briefing with Viper. The operation for his next contract would take place at the prosecutor's home just outside the city at precisely 1 AM. This meant he had roughly twelve hours to mentally wrap his brain around the next atrocity he would soon commit. Leon had hoped that a little bit of light exercise would clear his head, but the weight of what was asked of him still hung heavy on his conscience.

When it was finally time for target practice. Leon prepared his knives and gauged the distance and angle between him and the usual training dummy, as he had done so many times before. With how often Leon had practiced his knife throwing in this manner, this routine training should have been something he could easily perform while half-asleep.

Leon readied his first knife, struggling to steady his breath. He took a deep inhale before slowly letting the breath fade in a controlled exhale. In a quick, fluid motion, he threw the knife. The blade missed the training dummy by a few centimeters, the handle glancing off the matted wall a few feet behind it, and unceremoniously landing on the ground.

"Damn it…" Leon cursed under his breath.

He sighed, struggling to rein in the doubts and fears that currently ran wild in his head.

"Sloppy technique," a familiar voice groaned.

Leon turned around to the sight of Bullet standing behind him with a hand to her hip and brandishing a disappointed scowl.

"Are you even trying?" she asked pedantically.

Leon shot the sadistic sniper an annoyed glare. "What do you want, Bullet?" he asked.

"Nothing," Bullet scoffed. "I just came here on a hunch, thinking you'd still be tearing yourself apart after our last job."

She sneered.

"Lo' and behold, I was right."

Bullet briefly examined the knife on the floor with a side-eye glance before smugly smiling in contempt at Leon.

"My, my, how the mighty have fallen," she mused. "I think you might be washed up, Raven."

Leon's blood started to boil in agitation, slowly reaching a fever pitch the more Bullet ran her mouth.

"If this is the best you can do now, then you might as well take one of those knives and slit your own throat—"

"Shut up!" Leon barked.

"Oh, did I strike a nerve, lil birdie?" Bullet asked with rancid condescension.

Leon was barely able to restrain his rage, his voice dropping to a husky and guttural growl.

"I am not in the mood for your bullshit right now!" he snarled. "Unless you want me to take one of these knives and slit your throat in the most painful way possible! Leave me alone!"

Bullet shrugged. "Don't make promises you can't keep, babe," she said. "I shouldn't be wasting my time on a has-been assassin anyway."

Looking down upon him as if he were a cockroach, Bullet walked away while laughing to herself. Leon clenched his fists at his side, shaking in anger. In a furious blaze, he grabbed each of his remaining knives and hurled them at the training dummy. Each knife landed blade-first, the final one splintering the wood of the training dummy's head and knocking the fixture over onto the ground. Leon huffed, standing alone in silence, his heavy and trembling breaths only embellishing the painful quiet.

Bullet. Undertaker. Oblivion. Assassination. Simply existing. It all ate away at him like a corrosive acid. Every damn thing about the godforsaken world in which he lived pissed him off. If he didn't follow Undertaker's orders to the letter, the family who meant everything to him would be brutally murdered. If he went through his next contract, he'd never be able to look himself in the mirror, let alone show his face to Jamie and Lily. From every possible angle, the Black Bird of Death was cornered with no hope of escape. He was no different than an animal in a cage. Trapped, and utterly hopeless. Leon fell to his knees, trying desperately not to cry.

"I just want everything to disappear..." he quietly sobbed.

***

When Leon returned home that evening, he was a broken-down shell of a man. He went into his kitchen, took out the cheap bottle of bourbon he had saved for bad days, and filled a small glass halfway full. He pounded the drink no differently than you would a shot of tequila, swallowing the fiery liquid in one gulp. Leon gasped, wiping his lips, sitting down at his kitchen island while waiting for the booze to take the edge off of his misery.

Leon checked his watch. The time read 8:47 PM. Only a few more hours remained until he had to leave for his next job. Leon clutched his forehead with his left hand, trying to settle his racing thoughts. He had no choice but to see this through. He lost count of the number of people he killed for simple financial gain long ago. So many lives were ended directly by his hand. Leon had told himself time and time again that he was prepared to do anything to provide for and protect brother and sister, no matter how morally dubious, vile, or underhanded it might be. That's what a big brother was supposed to do. That was his one and only purpose in life. After all the terrible things he had done, the crimes he had committed, he couldn't just curl up and die while he still had something to live for. Otherwise, every sinful act that he had performed on behalf of his employer would have all been for nothing. But this next contract— the idea of ending the life of some innocent kid just to make a statement to his father for his client... Just the thought of going through with such an awful thing made Leon want to peel off his own skin and feed it to a wood chipper.

"Leon?" a voice called. "Are you okay?"

Leon flinched, startled by the sound. He noticed Lily standing in her bedroom door, staring at him with blatant concern and pity in her eyes. Leon let out a weak exhale, attempting to recompose himself for his sister's sake.

"Sorry, I didn't mean to jump like that," he mumbled. "It was a crappy day at work. I have a lot on my mind."

"I see..." Lily said, dejectedly looking away from Leon.

"Is Jamie home too?" Leon asked.

Lily shook her head. "No," she said. "He's over at a friend's place, but he said he'd be back before ten."

Leon stood up from his stool.

"Alright," he said. "I gotta head out to another work thing tonight, so I'll be out late. Don't wait for me for dinner."

Lily frowned. "Are you sure you're okay?" she asked once more.

"I'm fine," Leon replied bluntly.

"You just seem really on edge," Lily replied.

Leon crossed his arms, growing impatient.

"I'm fine," he curtly replied again. "Just focus on your studies—"

"That's enough, Leon!" Lily yelled.

Leon froze, startled by his sister's sudden outburst.

"I can't take it anymore!" she cried. "Please stop pushing us away!"

Lily bit her lip, desperately fighting through the hesitation that bound her for so long, and bulldozing it completely.

"You've been doing something incredibly illegal to make money all these years, haven't you?" she asked.

Leon grimaced. It was as if his entire world was crumbling around him. He didn't know what to say or what to do. Should he try to keep lying? Should he tell his sister everything? Every potential outcome left Leon terrified that any possible action he could take would make this hellish situation even worse.

"...How long have you known?" he finally asked in shame.

Lily looked down at the floor. "For a long time. You're honestly a crappy liar," she said. "Jamie and I have suspected for years now. We just didn't have the guts to confront you about it directly."

Leon didn't say a word.

"I won't ask you what you've been doing," Lily said. "I know you probably have a good reason to want to keep this a secret all these years, but please… Walk away from it!"

Leon frowned. "It's not that easy, Lily," he replied. "I'll handle everything—"

"Leon! Please!" Lily pleaded. "No amount of money is worth seeing you like this! You need to stop—"

"Do you think I take pleasure in this!?" Leon snapped. "Do you honestly think I wouldn't leave this all behind and live some easy-peasy life if I could!?"

Leon couldn't choke it down anymore. Every ounce of rage, every bit of turmoil and resentment he had swallowed over the years resurfaced. It was an old, festering, unhealed emotional wound that suddenly reopened and started bleeding again.

"Can you please cut me some god damn slack!" he screamed. "Our dad was a good-for-nothing deadbeat bastard who walked out on us! And our bleeding-heart of a mom died clinging to a pipe dream she was better off leaving behind! They made a fucking mess of our family and left me to pick up the pieces! I have torn myself apart inside and out trying to provide for you and Jamie! All I want more than anything is to be free from this— all of this awful bullshit chaining me down! And you and Jamie still have the nerve to act like it's somehow my fault I had to resort to becoming a criminal!"

Tears streamed down Lily's face as she angrily gritted her teeth.

"I don't want to be your guilty burden, Leon!" she retorted in an angry shout. "If that's how you feel, I'll start looking for a job and move out of here by the end of the month! Go do whatever the hell you want, you asshole! You're free now!"

Lily stormed off to her room, slamming her door behind her and locking it. The quiet only punctuated the sound of Leon's slow, heavy breaths. He was angry. He was actively being suffocated by guilt and loneliness, and more than anything, he deeply regretted snapping at Lily the way he just did. Leon's emotional and mental state was the human equivalent of a blazing dumpster fire. He was all but certain that the way he just took out his anger on Lily was making their mother roll in her grave.

"I'm sorry I'm such a crappy big brother…" he muttered quietly, completely ashamed of himself.

Utterly defeated, Leon checked his watch. He decided it would be for the best if he started getting ready for his next assignment. There was nothing more he could do, other than to give Lily some time to cool off. After all, Leon still needed to complete his next job for the sake of his brother and sister. He would apologize to Lily in the morning, and then figure out his next move after that.

Chapter 9

The prosecutor's home was in an upscale suburb on the city's outskirts. During the day, the neighborhood would have been teaming with people going about their peaceful daily lives, but it was so late into the night that almost everyone who lived there was now tucked away in their homes, fast asleep. The city streets were damp from a fresh rain, and were illuminated by the warm yellow glow of street lights.

After having arrived via the train, Leon carefully and quietly scoped the lonely roadways. He scoured the area, heading towards the home address that Viper had given him during his prior intelligence briefing. Leon buried the turmoil that raged and anguished deep within, attempting to numb himself to Lily's disappointment and the heinous act he would soon commit on behalf of Oblivion as well.

The residence of the prosecutor was a large townhouse, behind a tall and towering cast-iron fence with thick, dark black bars. The front gate was locked behind a four-digit code, and attempting to tamper with the mechanism or scale the perimeter would have tripped an alarm for a pricey private security service that the prosecutor paid for. Luckily, Viper had already secured the PIN code beforehand, and a handler had stashed a supply of knives in the off chance Leon needed them in the bushes of a nearby public park. All he had to do was open the front gate, sneak in, kill his mark, and sneak out. It was, by all means, a simple job that would be open and shut for an assassin of Leon's skill. He had carried out successful contracts in areas far more populated and heavily fortified, and yet, despite that knowledge, his current assignment left a paralyzing anxiety that pooled in his gut and continued to grow as the emotion piled up like chunky globs of sludge.

Leon cracked his knuckles, steeling his resolve. He input the PIN code into the keypad, the device making a quiet chirp in approval as the gate slowly slid open. Leon quietly and quickly made for the front stoop and hunched down at the front door. He tricked open the lock with a safety pin he stashed in his coat pocket, silently slipping inside and making his way up the stairs to the second floor. In the furthest room down the hall on the left-hand side was Charlie's bedroom. The door was cracked open, and Leon crept in, precisely and steadily pushing the door open without a sound.

The Black Bird of Death's latest target remained fast asleep in his bed with his covers tucked over his shoulders as he hugged a small stuffed teddy bear. He was eight years old, slightly small for his age, with fair skin and muddy brown hair. The boy's breaths were slow and peaceful, blissfully unaware of the intruder who now towered over him as if he were the shadow of the Grim Reaper.

Leon readied his knife, holding it carefully as he loomed over his target like a fearsome lion cornering a sleeping sheep.

Just take the knife and slide the blade across his throat... Leon thought to himself. *No different than a knife cutting through butter.*

Leon held the knife under Charlie's chin, quiet as a church mouse.

No chickening out!

As Leon tried to move his left hand closer to the boy's throat, his arm started to tremble. Leon used his right hand to hold his left forearm steady.

Just do it already!

Leon's guts were twisting themselves into a tight knot. As he tried to go through with what had to be done, he pictured both Lily and Jamie when they were small children. He imagined their voices in his head.

"*Leon's a monster!*" They both screamed in his mind's eye. "*Run away!*"

Leon clenched his jaw, trying once more to steal his resolve.

"*Leon's a monster!*"

"*Leon's a monster!*"

He clutched the handle of his knife in his hand, trying to tune his thoughts out as best he could. He couldn't fail. Now more than ever, he had to bury his feelings and get the job done.

"*Leon's a monster!*"

"*Leon's a monster!*"

"*Leon's a—*"

I CAN'T DO IT! Leon screamed internally.

The assassin was sick to his stomach. It took all of his strength not to fall to his knees. He had to get out of there. As silently and quietly as he broke into the prosecutor's home, the Black Bird of Death quickly vanished and ran off into the night, both angry and ashamed of his ever-growing weakness.

***

Leon sprinted down the quiet suburban streets. His mind was a chaotic hot mess, suffocated by a tangled and twisted web of self-loathing, doubt, desperation, confusion, and hopelessness. When he no longer had the strength to run anymore, he found himself in a public park that had closed after sundown. A gentle breeze delicately swayed the nearby swings, making a subtle creaking sound that faded into the night. A sound that was ultimately drowned out by the frantic buzzing of Leon's racing mind.

The air was brisk, and Leon had broken out in a cold sweat. He couldn't breathe, the weight of the world itself closing in upon him. His stomach churned violently, utterly overwhelmed by the adrenaline pumping through his veins—

"BLARGH!"

Leon promptly vomited into the lawn, dry heaving and gasping for air after the fact. He coughed and wheezed, desperately trying to regain control of his breathing. He fell on his back and into the dew-covered sod, the frigid moisture lightly soaking through his suit and prickling his skin like a dry needle. After a few minutes of heavy huffs, Leon managed to regain some semblance of control over his haywire emotions.

"I'm a failure..." he whispered into the wind.

Leon bore a thousand-yard stare as he gazed up into the night sky from the ground.

"I can't cut it as an assassin— let alone as a person... I'm pathetic..."

His chest tightened. Memories of the kills he had performed as the Black Bird of Death flashed before his eyes. Leon pictured the smiling faces of Jamie and Lily, and the horror and disgust he was certain they would feel if they knew the kind of feral beast their big brother truly was.

"I became a monster, and now I have nothing to show for it. If I don't figure something out right now, I am fucking screwed."

A twig snapped off in the bushes. Leon bolted upright, on full alert. From the corner of his eye, he saw a shadowy figure run off into the shadows.

"Shit!" Leon cursed, realizing that the humanoid form couldn't be anyone else but his assigned handler, who had just now witnessed his failure.

Leon sprang to his feet, sprinting after him. The Black Bird of Death pursued the agent to the street, where he mounted a motorcycle. The engine roared to life as the handler attempted to drive away.

"You're not going anywhere!" Leon barked.

Readying a knife, Leon threw it at lightning speed. The blade pierced the back of the handler's neck, the man letting out a muffled scream as he fell to the ground, not even able to drive more than a few feet away as he and his motorcycle fell to the ground. Leon darted over to his latest victim.

"Fuck! Fuck! Fuck!" he cried frantically over and over again.

Leon's heart was pounding out of his chest. He knew well that the handler he had just killed was likely not the only agent present. Oblivion had eyes and ears everywhere, and there was a very real possibility that Undertaker had already received word of his failure.

"Damn it!" he spat in stressed frustration, heaving the handler's body and tossing it to the side of the road.

Leon had to get home right away. Lily and Jamie were in great danger. He had to protect them. The Black Bird of Death mounted the deceased handler's motorcycle, tearing off at full speed into the night.

***

Leon pulled in front of his building, practically throwing his stolen vehicle aside in an anxious haze as he rushed upstairs to his apartment. He had no idea what he would do next, or how he could feasibly protect Lily and Jamie from Undertaker's wrath. He just had to get to them first and make sure they were safe. He'd figure out his plan as he went along, like any panicked person flying by the seat of their pants in a crisis situation would.

Please be okay! Please be okay! Leon repeated in his head over and over again.

When Leon reached his apartment unit, he saw that the lock was busted and the door was cracked open. The familiar and sickening smell of blood hung heavy in the air.

Leon gasped in horror. "No..." he quietly whimpered.

Leon scrambled inside. Jamie was lying in a pool of his own blood with a gunshot wound to his chest. His little brother's lifeless eyes stared into Leon's very soul.

"No... No... No!"

The reality was too cruel to even process. Leon frantically ran to Lily's half-open bedroom door, bursting inside. Lily was lying on the floor, shot in her stomach. She mustered all the strength she could to gaze upward at her big brother.

"Le... On..." she weakly called.

"Lily!" Leon cried, throwing himself to the floor.

Leon clutched Lily in his arms, desperately pressing his left hand against her stomach to stop the bleeding.

With all the strength she could muster, Lily reached out to her older brother.

"Leon... Help... me..." she quietly trembled.

Lily's hand fell to the ground.

"Lily! Please! Hold on!" Leon screamed.

The light left Lily's eyes. She remained still and stiff in her brother's arms.

"Lily..." he called. "Lily... Please don't leave me!"

His sister did not respond.

"Lily... Please wake up!"

Tears started to well up in Leon's eyes, dripping down onto the cheeks of Lily's corpse.

"Lily! Please don't go! Without you and Jamie... I— Please! Please wake up!"

Leon clenched his jaw, his torrential despair a raging storm that built up inside of him, clutching the body of his dear little sister in his arms even harder.

"Lily! Please wake up!" he sobbed. "Don't leave me!"

Everything The Black Bird of Death had fought for, everything he sacrificed his very soul for, his entire reason for living— it was all for nothing. Everything Leon Graves had held dear was obliterated beyond repair.

"LILY!"

Chapter 10

It had been two days since the Black Bird of Death's failure. Undertaker sat at a table in The Final Exit with Styx by his side, receiving a formal report from Viper on the matter.

"At 1:00 AM. An Oblivion agent, codenamed Raven, set off to fulfill his assigned contract," he reported. "At 1:12 AM. The assigned handler spotted Raven fleeing from the location of his contract, his target still alive. The handler followed Raven to a nearby public park, where he officially reported the operation's failure, and was then killed by Raven not long after."

Viper remained stiff, reporting the events of that night with a cold detachment that belied his emotional discomfort.

"1:21 AM. A preliminary contract was formally ordered. The targets were listed as Lily Graves, age nineteen, and Jamie Graves, age seventeen. They were both to be killed immediately."

Undertaker listened intently, with a cold, unflinching gaze that made it borderline impossible to discern what was going through his head.

"1:29 AM, an Oblivion agent that was assigned on standby set out to fulfill the contract taken out on Lily and Jamie Graves. 1:32 AM. Oblivion agent, codenamed Bullet, broke into the apartment unit where the designated targets lived. At 1:42 AM, the contract was reported by its handler to have been completed successfully."

"And where do things stand now?" Undertaker shrewdly asked.

"The bodies of Lily and Jamie Graves were officially discovered and reported two days ago, between 8 and 9 AM, by one of their neighbors. Authorities have since begun their initial investigation," Viper answered. "There were no eyewitnesses who saw Bullet anywhere near the scene of the crime, and the building lacked any security cameras. The odds of the crime being traced back to Oblivion in any meaningful way are minimal at best."

Viper bit his lip.

"However, Leon Graves, also known as the Oblivion Agent code-named Raven, has been declared missing and is currently considered the primary suspect in the murder of his siblings. Intelligence agents were able to gather that Raven returned to his home and discovered the bodies of his brother and sister shortly after Bullet had finished the job, but his whereabouts afterward are still unknown. At this time, Raven's status is listed as MIA, and he has officially been designated a traitor to Oblivion."

Viper bowed his head.

"This concludes my report, sir."

Undertaker sighed. "Very well." Undertaker's eyes flickered towards Styx. "Assign another agent to carry out the contract Raven failed to complete. Also, send out an APB for all Oblivion assassins who are not presently assigned to a job. If spotted, they are to kill the Black Bird of Death on sight. Whoever successfully brings him down will be rewarded handsomely. Anyone who aids him will also be declared a traitor to the organization and dealt with accordingly."

Viper grimaced, hesitant to speak, but giving in to the urge to do so anyway.

"Are you sure this is wise, sir?" he asked. "This is the Black Bird of Death we're talking about. We could have killed him and been done with it. But now... We may have unleashed the rage of one of the most feared assassins to—"

"Are you questioning my judgment?" Undertaker asked coldly.

Viper froze. "I— uh…" he stammered.

"You know, it would be an awful shame if someone were to leak some of Seraphim Pharmaceuticals' unsavory secrets to the press. Why your father would be absolutely ruined," Undertaker dryly mused. "But perhaps I simply misheard you."

Viper got down on his knees.

"I apologize, sir," he whimpered. "I humbly ask for your forgiveness. It won't ever happen again."

Undertaker stood up, standing above Viper and looking down upon him like he was some pathetic mongrel in human clothes.

"Hmph! Let the fate of the Black Bird of Death serve as an example to those who would question or defy me," he declared. "I will reward loyalty and successful results. But failure and disobedience will result in the absolute destruction of everything you hold dear."

Undertaker's cold glare shook Viper to his very core.

"Do you understand?" Undertaker asked.

Viper bowed his head.

"I understand…" he replied.

Undertaker smugly smirked. "Good," he sneered. "Now fuck off."

Undertaker walked towards the door. "Come styx," he ordered. "It's time we left this place."

Styx nodded in silent affirmation before briefly addressing Viper.

"If you should learn of any new developments concerning Raven, contact us immediately," she advised. "Farewell."

With that, Styx and her master departed, leaving Viper a groveling mess on the floor.

***

Later that night, Viper retreated to a back room in The Final Exit. He had fashioned it into a workshop, where various specimens of plant and animal materials were stored and studied. Viper came from a long line of assassins specializing in the use of poison. His clan's founders were assassins who acted as apothecaries, serving as both a front to conceal their activities and a means of financing their seedier ventures. It was only fitting that in the modern day, his family would run one of the most influential pharmaceutical companies in the entire world. After all, the line between miraculous medicine and deadly poison was thin and blurry at best.

Viper would always retreat to this workshop after a long day. Experimenting and creating new formulas for deadly substances, understanding their properties, and concocting various methods for these beautiful innovations to be effectively administered and utilized. For Viper, toxicology was straightforward. Simple. A science that followed a specific set of rules that were immutable to superfluous influences like money, status, or power. It was a source of comfort.

Viper reached below the counter and pulled out a mortar and pestle from a drawer. There were far more efficient methods to extract venom and toxins from materials, but for Viper, the old-fashioned way of doing things made him feel closer to his clan's roots. He rummaged through his various specimens before settling on plant bulbs to work with that evening. They were bulbs of the flower, *Lyrcoris radiata*, more commonly known as the red spider lily.

The bulbs of these flowers contained a toxic alkaloid known as lycorine. A toxin that, when ingested, could result in nausea, diarrhea, vomiting, convulsions, and, in high enough quantities, death. While this poison could also be found in other flower bulbs that were members of the same genus, Viper chose to work with this particular specimen for a rather whimsical reason. In flower language, the red spider lily symbolized death, remembrance, suffering, and sorrowful partings. He found great poetic beauty in using such a lovely blossom to create another marvelous instrument of death.

He smiled like a joyful little kid, using the pestle to crush the bulbs into a fine paste within the mortar. While doing so, Viper calculated in his head the dosage amounts he would start with during his initial round of testing, while also deliberating which type of animal would prove to be the most effective subject in which to study the effects of the poison—

Without warning, the lights shut off.

"Son of a…" Viper groaned.

Viper stood in the darkened room, grumbling in annoyance as he carefully tried to place the pestle on his workbench without dropping it on the floor. Viper's eyes had not yet adjusted to the shadows, and he could barely see beyond his nose. He crossed his arms in frustration, knowing full well that his productivity would be heavily stifled attempting to continue to work in the middle of a blackout.

"Good evening, Viper," a voice called.

Before he had a chance to respond, Viper heard a loud snap and, suddenly, a sharp pain shot through his heel. He howled in agony, falling to the ground. A throwing knife stuck out from Achilles' tendon, seething in hellish pain as his fight or flight instinct kicked into overdrive.

"Raven! Is that you!?" he asked in a scream, practically gritting his teeth.

Viper couldn't make out the details of his assailant. All he could discern was the faint outline of someone's feet in the darkness and the odor of dirt and dried blood that clung to them and hung heavy in the air.

"It's me, alright," Leon mused, almost intoxicated by his pure manic energy. "With all the Oblivion dipshits hounding me right now, I feel like fucking big shot!"

Viper desperately tried in vain to climb to his feet, his right leg fully unable to hold his body's weight, causing him to fall over while his senses were overwhelmed by pain.

"What the hell is wrong with you!? What do you think you're doing!?" he asked.

"Isn't it obvious? I'm here to kill you." Leon replied bluntly.

Viper's eyes widened in shock. "Why!?" he shouted.

"Why?" Leon parroted back.

Leon chuckled. That small chuckle slowly morphed into mirthless laughter that grew louder and louder.

"Ahahahaha! Don't you remember the little chat we had a few days ago?" He scoffed. "The one about how if someone were to hurt the loved ones of an assassin, he'd find the bastards responsible and make them pay."

Viper froze as if he were a frightened woodland creature staring death in the face.

"You lot took **everything** from me!" Leon roared, his voice dropping to a raspy and angry growl. "I became a cold-hearted monster for the sake of the people I cared about more than anything! I sold my soul to Undertaker and Oblivion! And you bastards still had the nerve to say it wasn't good enough!"

Viper cowered in fear, unable to run away. He realized in that moment that this was the inevitable outcome of Undertaker having chosen to flex on the Black Bird of Death, all for the sake of his petty sadism and control. His love for his family was the only thing that ever kept Leon from turning against the organization that exploited him, and now they unleashed the savage beast within. There was absolutely nothing anyone could do now to seal it away once more.

"And now it's your turn," Leon snarled. "I will hunt down every person responsible for Jamie and Lily's deaths, and they will die by my hand."

Viper trembled on the ground. "I— I was just following orders!" he stammered. "I— I was just doing what Undertaker asked me to do! Please! Please don't kill me! Please! I— I'm begging you—"

"Are you fucking serious!?" Leon spat. "You're really begging for life right now!? Have some god damn self-respect!"

Viper saw the blade of a knife faintly gleam in the shadows.

"Do you know how many times I've heard a target beg for their life while carrying out a contract for Oblivion?" he asked. "Do you really think there was ever a time when that shit worked on me?"

"I was just following orders!" Viper cried once more.

"So you already said, but frankly, I don't give a damn," Leon replied. "Action. Inaction. Compliance. Rebellion. Like it or not, every decision we make has consequences."

The Black Bird of Death's shadow loomed over Viper, his voice a songbird's requiem that heralded imminent demise.

"You sold them out. You're the one who provided Undertaker the intel needed to end Jamie and Lily's lives, and that's why I'm here to kill you."

Viper cowered on the floor. He couldn't fight back. He couldn't run away. The poison-obsessed intelligence agent was helpless prey that was about to be eviscerated by an apex predator.

"Like it or not, you reap what you sow, you damn dirty snake," Leon growled.

Tears streamed down Viper's face, practically pissing himself in sheer panic. Like a strike of lightning from the heavens on high, a knife was thrown into Viper's throat. He fell to the floor, choking on his own blood as the crimson liquid pooled on the ground. For a few mere moments, Viper's life flashed before his eyes, and then the light left them entirely. Leon looked down upon his corpse in frigid disappointment and disgust.

"And unfortunately for you… Your seeds were weak."

Chapter 11

Undertaker's private compound. A mansion located outside the city, secluded in its own large parcel of land. The abode was heavily fortified, with a concrete wall barrier built around the immediate perimeter of the estate. The location was teeming with heavily armed security personnel who were made up of both those who directly served Oblivion and those who served as independent private military contractors. On the third floor of the manor, where Undertaker's primary personal office was located, he received a report concerning the Black Bird of Death.

"At least twenty Oblivion agents have been found dead," Styx said. "Each one died as a result of sharp force trauma, indicative of being attacked by a single assailant with a knife."

Undertaker smoked a cigar while sitting at this desk, shrewdly assessing every word of Styx's report.

"Furthermore, an Oblivion storage facility was also breached. Four guardsmen were killed, and it was reported that the culprit made off with several explosive devices."

Undertaker's eyes narrowed into a cold glare. "...Is that all of the casualties?" he asked.

Styx bit her lip, her usual stoic expression showing a subtle hint of apprehension. She was reluctant to answer the question, but did so anyway out of an almost machine-like sense of duty.

"Viper's body was also found at The Final Exit," she reported. "He was found with a knife in his throat. His carotid artery was pierced, and he died of blood loss. Our preliminary investigation suggests that the culprit had shut off the power to the cafe, and then broke in to assassinate Viper during the blackout."

Undertaker glowered at Styx, the intensity of his gaze growing as she continued with her report.

"Based on Viper's involvement with the contracts taken out on Jamie and Lily Graves, and the manner in which he assassinated. We are operating under the likely conclusion that the culprit was none other than the Black Bird of Death."

"And his current location?" Undertaker callously probed.

"We're still trying to pinpoint his whereabouts, sir," Styx said, bowing her head in apology. "This is all I have to report at this time."

Undertaker remained ominously quiet after Styx had finished her report. Her head remained bowed as she waited for her next order, unsure how her superior would respond to the news of repeated failure after failure.

Undertaker finally let out a frustrated sigh. "It seems that the Black Bird of Death has decided to fully bare his talons against the organization," he mused. "How unfortunate…"

He stood up from behind his desk and walked towards the large window, gazing upon his vast estate.

"He was a fine operative until this point, and many clients were prepared to offer hefty sums to have the Black Bird of Death personally carry out a contract. I would have expected nothing less from the offspring of Fenrir…"

Styx raised her head. "You mean the Runaway Lone Wolf?" she asked.

Undertaker quietly chuckled, returning his attention to Styx.

"Yes, that's the one," he replied. "I'm curious… What do you know of him, Styx?"

Styx cleared her throat, standing tall and reciting her knowledge on the subject as she would any other report.

"I was just a grunt working with Intelligence at the time, but I've heard the stories," she replied. "Fenrir was an Oblivion agent who went MIA during a contract twenty-four years ago. His location remained unknown for a decade, his defection practically becoming an urban legend. Oblivion eventually found him living under the forged identity, Marshal Graves. It was at that point, he stormed a training facility and was killed after assassinating fifty other agents."

"'Assassinated' doesn't even begin to describe that shit show," Undertaker stated grimly. "It was a fucking bloodbath. The work of a suicidal maniac who was determined to take down as many people as he could along with him."

Undertaker wistfully smirked, almost nostalgically.

"Imagine how shocked I was when our investigations uncovered that Fenrir had married a civilian woman and had three children," he mused.

Styx's shoulders stiffened.

"May I ask a question, sir?" she asked.

"You may," Undertaker replied.

Styx nodded, briefly bowing once more in gratitude.

"With standard Oblivion protocol, why was his family ultimately left alive, sir?" she asked. "I'm familiar with Raven's connections to the man and how he came to become an agent for Oblivion, but why was he not killed all those years ago?"

Undertaker shrugged. "I considered it an investment," he replied. "I was curious. Would the progeny of the Fenrir, one of the greatest assassins to ever grace the criminal underworld, have inherited the skills and potential of his father?"

Undertaker returned to sit at his desk.

"In the end, it proved to be a worthwhile gamble, or at least it did. The Black Bird of Death eclipsed even Fenrir in skill, and thought only of the family he was obligated to provide for. A nobody society left to rot in the gutter. He was desperate. Easy to manipulate."

Undertaker clasped his hands on his desk, leaning forward.

"Honestly, after all the money he's made for me, I would have been tempted to give him a second chance, at least if he were to throw himself at my feet and grovel for forgiveness."

His face twisted to a cold scowl.

"But the Black Bird of Death has fully chosen defiance over obedience. Without exception, I will crush any fool who dares to bear their fangs against the hand that feeds them, and by extension, destroy everything they hold dear. I am the one in control, and I will use any method at my disposal to remind would-be traitors of that, no matter how excessive or vile."

Undertaker looked down upon Styx.

"Track down the Black Bird of Death, and kill him by any means necessary," he ordered. "I don't care what it takes. His insolence will not be tolerated. There is no escape from Oblivion, and all those who betray the organization will be dealt with accordingly. I will settle for nothing less than his head on a spike."

***

"Time to work, time to work," Bullet quietly chimed to herself, "Another day, another bullet to someone's brain."

Bullet stood on the rooftop of a twenty-story building. The brisk night air tickled her skin and was almost as invigorating as the kill she was about to perform. Her current job wasn't anything special. A contract was placed on a CEO with shady connections and ambitions for political office, and another party wanted him dead. The who and why of a kill never really interested Bullet much. As far as she was concerned, assassination itself was a blissful pleasure, and she was getting paid to do what she loved. The mad sniper had a fever, and the only cure was yet another murder.

Bullet assembled her darling little rifle, Oscar, taking stock of the wind direction and distance for her shot. Her target would be set meet with a certain illicit contact of his at a nearby parking garage, and her task would be to shoot them both down. The job was simple, and yet she prayed it would prove more satisfying than the two recent operations she was hired to carry out.

As she attached her scope to Oscar, she thought back to her job with the Black Bird of Death and the silencing of various defectors from Oblivion who banded together. It had all the potential to be something special, and recalling the sight of their heads exploding when she shot them down still made Bullet flush with mild excitement. Yet, during what should have been the final climax, Raven failed to perform. A man who was supposed to be a perfect instrument of death hesitated, and she had to take matters into her own hands.

Her most recent contract wasn't any better. Just two normie kids whom Undertaker wanted killed discreetly and efficiently. The boy tried to play hero to protect his dear sister, and practically shoved himself into the muzzle of her gun. The girl was even less thrilling, because she locked herself in her room like a pathetic, cowering kitten. The only satisfaction Bullet got from the job was that she left the girl bleeding out, and that her death was slow and painful.

"It's showtime," Bullet quietly mused.

She loaded her rifle and got down on the ground, peering through her scope once more to hunt her prey. The thrill of the chase. The beauty of spewing blood and tearing sinew. The look of absolute despair in her victim's eyes during their final moments. Killing was the only thing that made Bullet feel alive. It was a thrill that not even sex could live up to. She licked her lips in anticipation—

"The fuck!?" Bullet cursed in startled bafflement.

Through her scope, Bullet saw her targets, and both of them were lying dead on the parking garage floor with knives sticking out of their backs.

"Lovely night, isn't it?" a voice called.

Before she realized it was even happening, an assailant grabbed Bullet from behind and held her tightly against their chest, pressing a knife to her throat. She couldn't see the bastard's face, but they reeked of sweat, dirt, and blood.

"I took the liberty of carrying out your contract for you. I didn't want any distractions," a familiar voice whispered in her ear.

"Raven!" Bullet hissed. "What the hell are you doing?! Let me go!"

Leon chuckled. "Come on, no need to play hard to get. I thought you were into this? Killing and violence, I mean."

Bullet angrily ground her teeth as Leon pressed the knife against her throat.

"What's this about, bird brain?!" she spat.

Leon's grip around her torso tightened.

"Your last contract. What was it?" Leon asked.

"The hell does that have to do with anything—"

Leon pressed the blade of his knife against Bullet's throat with just enough pressure that it almost broke the skin.

"Tell me!" he ordered in a deep raspy growl.

"It was absolutely boring," Bullet hissed. "Just two dull kids Undertaker asked me to kill in their apartment in the dead of night. Why would he personally take out a contract on two lame-ass randos like that, I have no Idea—"

"Their names were Jamie and Lily! You fucking cow!" Leon roared.

Bullet smirked in dumbfounded and amused disbelief.

"What? Were they friends of yours?" she mockingly asked. "Your little brother and sister, perhaps?"

Leon remained deadly silent while Bullet cackled.

"Ahahaha! I get it now! So this is why you went and defected, huh? You're starting some pointless crusade against Oblivion to atone for their deaths! How adorable! You really are a pathetic washed-up assassin!"

The wind howled against the rooftop.

"Atone?" Leon scoffed. "I ain't atoning for shit. I crossed the point of no return a long time ago."

Bullet was baffled. "Then why go through with this?" she asked. "You can't defeat Oblivion! Even if you were to somehow kill Undertaker, someone else would just take his place—"

"Just shut the hell up, will you?" Leon growled. "I know all of that already."

The moonlight glistened and gleamed against Leon's knife.

"You'd think I would have some good reason to go through with all of this, but the truth is I don't have one... In the end, this is all nothing more than petty revenge."

Bullet's eyes widened. "...Revenge?"

"I'm gonna let you in on a little secret, Bullet," Leon said. "In this world, there's nothing more dangerous than a broken man with something to prove and nothing to live for."

Leon loomed over Bullet, his breath warm against the nape of her neck while whispering into her ear.

"You, Viper, and Undertaker took away my reason for living, so what does it matter if I die, right? But I still have some unfinished business before I kick the bucket. This was never about justice or redemption. I just want to find the scumbags who killed my brother and sister, and make them bleed, that's all. It doesn't matter how many people I have to kill or how many more crimes I have to commit. I won't be satisfied until Viper, you, and Undertaker are all dead by my hand."

Leon's grasp was a dastardly embrace.

"You always got off to killing and violence, practically getting wet as you watched your victims writhe in pain and agony in their final moments. Tell me… How does it feel to be on the receiving end for once?"

Bullet gulped. Her heart raced. A feeling she had long forgotten pooled in her chest, making her feel sick to her stomach. For the first time she could remember, Bullet feared for her life.

"Make sure to give Viper my regards, k? I'll see you in Hell, bitch."

Like a knife cutting through butter, Leon's knife danced across Bullet's throat in an elegant and dramatic slash. Her blood spewed and splattered in the pale glow of the moonlight as she fell to the ground. Once one of the most feared and deadly snipers in Oblivion's arsenal, in that moment, she was reduced to nothing more than yet another tally mark on the Black Bird of Death's ever-growing body count.

Chapter 12

"Sir, I regret to inform you that ten more agents who were pursuing the Black Bird of Death have been killed."

It was late in the afternoon. Undertaker sat behind his desk at his personal compound, receiving yet another report of failure from his loyal assistant, and head of Oblivion intelligence, Styx. Despite her stoic expression, an aura of shame weighed down on her. Based on the tone of her voice, it was a marvel Styx hadn't chosen to deliver her report while on her hands and knees, begging for forgiveness and mercy.

"Moreover, we have received a report from intelligence agents out in the field that Bullet was murdered while she was on an assignment," Styx explained. "Our preliminary investigation suggests that she and the handler were both killed by the Black Bird of Death, who also eliminated her designated target."

Styx bit her lip.

"A note was also left behind with Bullet's body."

Undertaker raised his head, turning his nose up at Styx.

"...What did it say?" he asked.

Styx's apprehension slowly and surely etched its way into her face like cracks forming in a stone statue.

"It simply said, 'you're next,'" she answered.

A cold fury boiled in Undertaker's blood. His eyes strained themselves into menacing slits, his icy and piercing glare chilling Styx to her core.

"Let me see if I understand the situation correctly," he quietly growled.

Undertaker stretched his right hand on his desk, cracking and popping his knuckles as his rage began to boil over.

"Five days… In roughly five days, one singular man has stolen valuable supplies from Oblivion, killed more than thirty Oblivion agents, killed one of our best intelligence officers and go-to poison specialist, killed our best sniper, and issued a formal threat against my life. Yet, he remains alive with his current whereabouts completely unknown?"

Styx trembled at the sight of her master, who looked upon her as if he were a cold-hearted arbiter and executioner.

"Sir! We're doing everything we can—"

"Yes or no?" Undertaker interjected with a frigid bite. "Answer the question."

Styx clenched her hands into fists at her sides.

"Yes," she replied, grimacing from the sour taste of shame and fear that pervaded her tongue.

Undertaker opened one of his desk top drawers.

"Sir, we just need some more time," Styx assured. "I promise we'll capture the Black Bird of Death very soon, we just need to—"

BANG!

She never even saw it coming. A bullet pierced Styx's skull, the force of which caused the upper right half of her head to explode. Her brain matter and skull fragments scattered like shrapnel. Styx's soul departed the world of the living before her body even hit the floor. Undertaker held a pistol in his right hand, recoiling in annoyed contempt at his assistant's corpse with a disgust that could only belong to a narcissistic man who fancied himself a divine being.

"Absolutely fucking useless…" he groaned. "Every last one of them."

Undertaker got out of his chair and stepped over the window that overlooked his estate.

"The Black Bird of Death is more than welcome to *try* and kill me, but his efforts will be in vain," he scoffed.

Undertaker's estate was heavily fortified. The property had been built in a relatively remote location. Security cameras overlooked just about every nook and crevice of the place, and it was swarming with security personnel who were all under Undertaker's direct employment, many of whom were former soldiers and private military contractors. Even the Black Bird of Death, whose primary specialty was in infiltration and covert assassination, would be hard-pressed to make it inside, let alone successfully reach Undertaker to kill him. The CEO of Oblivion even had the foresight to have a hidden underground passage way built, should he ever need to evacuate the premises on a moment's notice.

Undertaker let out a deep sigh, stepping away from the window and over towards Styx's body, and shaking his head.

"I suppose, for a moment there, I might have lost my composure…" he thought aloud. Getting this mess properly cleaned up will take some time, and I'll have to hire a new assistant. Oh well. It was good stress relief if nothing else."

Leon Graves. Oblivion agent code name: Raven. The assassin known in many circles as the Black Bird of Death. A killing prodigy and son of the Runaway Lone Wolf. Once a profitable asset to the organization, picturing his face now caused Undertaker to seethe in a quiet and white hot burning fury.

"I will remain in control," he proclaimed. "This world is one where only the strong come out on top. Those with money and power survive and make rules, while those who don't rot and die. I am at the top of this food chain, and no one will ever change that."

***

Later that night, relaxing in a lounge located in the eastern wing of his estate, Undertaker savored a scotch on the rocks. It had been a long day for the CEO of Oblivion. Failure after failure from his subordinates wore thin on his patience, and now the Black Bird of Death had the nerve to threaten his life directly.

As he sat in a leather armchair worth more money than many would ever earn in their lifetime, with his gun placed on a nearby end table, he glanced out into the night and took in his vast property illuminated under the light of the full moon. Undertaker had resolved to remain at his compound for the time being and let Leon Graves get himself killed trying to break in. After all, why bother chasing someone who's hunting you down? Undertaker had an earpiece so he could get reports directly from his security suite, and he had two formidable bodyguards standing directly outside his door, who were to protect him at all times. He swished his drink lightly, the ice cubes making a quiet tapping sound against the sides of the glass before taking another sip—

BOOM!

Undertaker bolted out of his chair, his glass shattering on the floor as he dropped it to the ground. Outside his window, a raging inferno blazed at the front gate.

Undertaker's earpiece made a faint chirp. "Intruder alert!" a security agent shouted. "There's been an explosion! All available personnel to the main gate now!"

"Requesting back up!" another agent desperately barked. "We've engaged the intruder, but he has already killed five men! I repeat! Requesting— **AHHHHHH!**"

The agent screamed in agony as his voice was silenced with the loud hiss of radio static.

"What are you idiots doing!?" Undertaker spat. "Kill the intruder now! I don't care what it takes! Just do it!"

One by one, Undertaker heard the voices of his men being silenced by their attacker, their screams growing bloodier and bloodier as the chaos spiraled out of control.

BOOM!

Another explosion went off, rattling the estate and shutting down the power. The sound echoed into the distance. Undertaker's earpiece remained ominously silent.

"Give me a status report! Now!" Undertaker barked.

There was no response.

"Status report!"

There was no answer. Undertaker felt a cold sweat that was now slowly beating down the back of his neck. He could hear the sounds of screams outside that were muffled by the walls, progressively growing quieter the longer the situation played out. Undertaker grabbed his handgun off the end table, scrambling while he switched off the firearm's safety and aimed it at the door. If the Black Bird of Death was going to be brazen enough to storm his front door, he would shoot him the moment he entered.

Undertaker held his gun steady, his breath short and shallow. He heard his guards fall to the ground outside with a loud thud, both of them letting out a stifled shout. Footsteps echoed from down the hallway outside, slowly growing louder as they approached. Undertaker held his finger to the gun's trigger, ready to fire at any moment. The footsteps stopped outside his door. Undertaker held his breath. The intense silence was reminiscent of a calm before the storm.

The door burst open, and before he could pull the trigger, a sharp shooting pain shot through his right hand.

"God damn it!" he screamed.

A knife impaled Undertaker's right hand, knocking his gun to the ground. He fell to one knee, grunting in anguish, blood dripping down from his wounds and onto the floor. The blade struck cleanly through the back of his right hand and lightly gouged the palm of his left.

"Did you miss me?" a familiar voice coyly asked.

Leon Graves stood in the doorway, his form illuminated by the red glow of the flames outside. His face was covered in dirt, along with both dried and fresh blood, his long crimson hair a tangled mane of fire. Leon's suit was torn to shreds, his green eyes were beady, and he brandished a manic grin. The Black Bird of Death looked like a demon that crawled straight out of a war-torn battlefield in Hell.

"What's wrong? Are you afraid?" he taunted.

"Shut up!" Undertaker spat.

Getting back to his feet, Undertaker charged at Leon, shoving the Black Bird of Death into the wall with his shoulder. He ran away down the hall after narrowly avoiding tripping over the bodies of his security guards. Leon sauntered after his former boss at a leisurely pace.

"I was expecting a little bit more, y'know?" he called. "It's kind of a disappointment, honestly. It turns out that without your money or power, you're just another weak lil rat like the rest of us."

Undertaker ran to his cellar, making for the emergency escape route he had built specifically for a situation like this. He sprinted down a flight of stairs into his manor's main foyer, bodies littering the floor of the darkened room.

"Go ahead and run! I want to savor every little moment right now!"

Undertaker made for the kitchen, and when he got there, he found his personal chef was dead on the kitchen tile with his throat slit.

"I want you to suffer! I want to see absolute terror and despair in your eyes when I kill you!"

Undertaker rushed to open the cellar door with his left hand and ran down the stairs to the basement. The cellar contained tall shelves that stored various cooking ingredients such as raw flour, dried spices, and various kitchen implements. Undertaker rushed over to the back corner of the cellar, where, under a removable tile, was a trap door to a secret tunnel outside. He would escape and live to see another day, no matter what. He would—

"God fucking damn it!"

A knife stuck out of the back of Undertaker's thigh. He screeched in pain through his clenched teeth, desperately trying to stand back up, but falling back to his knees.

"Gotcha," Leon playfully chimed with a smirk and a sadistic glint in his eyes.

Leon slinked to one of the storage shelves that housed several large sacks of flour. One by one, he used a knife to gouge a hole into each sack and tossed it with seeming reckless abandon. The white powder scattered and polluted the air.

"It was a good thing you sent so many agents after me," he mused. "There were a few I held up at knife point, and I told them that I would spare their lives if they gave me any info about you and your fancy estate. That's how I learned about your lil escape hatch down here."

He laughed, tossing yet another sack of flour.

"It was all a lie, of course. I was gonna kill 'em either way. I just wanted to see if I get any useful intel out of it first."

Undertaker attempted to crawl away, dragging his body across the floor towards his emergency exit.

"And where do you think you're going?" Leon called.

He quickly bent down and picked up a clump of flour on the floor, circling in front of Undertaker. With a heavy and theatrical thrust of his arm, he threw the flour into his former employer's face. Undertaker coughed and gagged; choking on the flour as it burst into a big white puff. Leon casually flipped Undertaker onto his back with the flick of his wrist and pinned Undertaker under his foot.

"Let me go! You ungrateful bastard!" Undertaker spat.

"Oh? What have you done for me that I should be grateful for?" Leon asked, playfully tilting his head.

"I made you!" Undertaker roared. "I was the one who propelled the reputation of the Black Bird of Death! I am the reason you were one of the most high-profile and sought-after killers ever! Were it not for me, you and your pathetic lil family would have starved out in the gutter!"

Leon rolled his eyes.

"Is that really something so worthy of gratitude?" He asked. "I provided you a service, and you paid me for it. I don't believe in rewarding people for what should be basic human decency. Besides…"

Leon ground the heel of his shoe into Undertaker's sternum like he was a cock roach. Undertaker gasped and groaned, the pressure the Black Bird of Death applied almost making it hard to breathe.

"I performed kill after kill for Oblivion. I became a monster for Oblivion. I pushed away and neglected my brother and sister— my entire reason for becoming tangled up in your web of bullshit, for Oblivion… And you still had the fucking nerve to ask for more!"

The flour wafted through the air, filling the cellar with a dusty haze.

"It's funny, though. If you settled for just killing me, you probably could have saved yourself from all this trouble."

Leon stomped his foot into Undertaker's ribcage, reveling in his former boss's screams.

"Yet you had to have absolute control over me, and every last person working under you!" he snarled, stomping his foot into Undertaker's ribcage over and over again. "You just had to set an example for everyone else by getting Lily and Jamie involved! You egotistical asshole!"

Leon lifted his foot off Undertaker's chest, Undertaker beaten bloody, coughing, and gasping for air.

"But hey, it's all okay as long as you stay ahead on your bottom line!" he mused. "That's just capitalism for you!"

He picked up Undertaker by his shirt collar, clenching the fabric in a tight and merciless grip. Leon held his former boss up close to his face, Undertaker utterly dwarfed by the manic rage that boiled behind the broken assassin's eyes.

"It doesn't matter how many awful things you do. It doesn't matter how many people you have to screw over. Even if the sea of dead bodies piles up past your neck, it's all hunky-dory as long as you can turn a profit from it, right?"

Leon's expression was unhinged and filled with malice as he leered into Undertaker's soul.

"Hell, even after I kill you, I'm sure Oblivion will just carry on like normal, like nothing ever happened. Shitty people will pay good money to have other shitty people killed. There's a profit to be made, and those who stand to benefit from it aren't gonna stop just because it's morally wrong. I wouldn't be surprised if there were at least ten people who are chomping at the bit to get your job."

Leon tossed Undertaker back on the ground. The black bird of death ran his fingers through his long red hair, almost taking on a dissonant serenity.

"You know, in a weird way, though... I should be thanking you. This little petty quest of revenge... It was all for me. The dead are beyond suffering. Whether or not I avenge their deaths— it doesn't really mean much to Lily and Jamie now, does it?"

He gave a warm chuckle.

"This was the first time in my life I actually did something for myself for once. It was kind of nice... fucked up, and twisted as it was."

Leon took a deep breath, stifling a small cough as he choked on the flour in the air for a brief moment.

"Believe it or not, when I was a kid, I always wanted to be a baker," he said. "As you can clearly see, the dream didn't exactly pan out."

Leon theatrically gestured both his hands towards the various emptied flour sacks on the floor, their contents now polluting the air of the cramped cellar.

"Flour is a staple ingredient in baking, y'know. But it can be surprisingly dangerous under the right circumstances."

Undertaker stared at Leon in confusion, his heart racing.

"What the hell does that have to do with anything?" he asked.

Leon stretched out his right arm, cracking his shoulder.

"Well, you see, a little fun fact you might not know is that when flour is finely sifted and aerosolized, it becomes highly flammable," he explained. "Just a little spark could set it all ablaze."

Leon pulled a cigarette lighter from his pocket.

"In a tight and enclosed area like this, why wouldn't it be much different than lighting a match by a gas leak, wouldn't you say?"

Undertaker's gasped in horror. "No! Don't!" he screeched. "I'll do anything!"

Leon took a deep breath, closing his eyes.

"I'll see you in Hell, Undertaker," he declared.

Leon held up the lighter in his left hand, holding his thumb against the trigger.

"NO!" Undertaker screamed.

With a small click, Leon lit the cigarette lighter. In a mere instant, the flour was lit ablaze and exploded outward. Undertaker and Leon were blown across the room while the flames danced and scattered all around. When Leon opened his eyes, he was lying on the floor. He was severely burned, the billowing embers holding him tightly in their lovely embrace. He couldn't feel his arms and legs, and his vision was starting to blur now that he found himself on the brink of death. A few feet away, Undertaker had hit the wall headfirst, his skull shattering on impact.

Leon smiled, practically giddy. As he took his final breaths, he was the happiest he had ever been. This world was full of rotten people who preyed upon those whom they saw as their lessers, all while bystanders simply let it happen over and over again. Meanwhile, everyone who was deemed useless to society, one way or another, was left to rot in the gutter without a second thought. It was an existence he had come to loathe with every fiber of his being— but soon... Soon, that wouldn't be any of his problem. Leon's suffering and pain were about to come to an end. That burden would not be his to bear any longer, and he would be released from the endless cycle of misery and sorrow that entrapped him. Everything would finally be over because, by dying, Leon Graves found his only means of escape.

The Black Bird of Death would soon be free from his cage.

About the Author

Michael Emond is an author born and raised in Northeast Ohio. A self-described workaholic, if he's not reading, playing video games, or watching anime, he's either brainstorming or working on a new creative project.

www.ingramcontent.com/pod-product-compliance
Lightning Source LLC
LaVergne TN
LVHW061555070526
838199LV00077B/7063